WINTER

CALLING

VIRGINIA CLAN

Forevermore

Blessed Twice

Imagining Reality

Wasted Heart

At Last

ASPEN FRIENDS

Life Rewired

Something So Grand

Mending Defects

OTHER ROMANCES

Winter Calling

Out of Order

Clichéd Love

One-Off

Full Court Pressure

Uncommon Emotions

WINTER

CALLING

LYNN GALLI

PENIKILA PRESS

ISBN: 978-1-935611-10-3

Printed in the United States of America.

SYNOPSIS

Sometimes, working at a ski resort feels more like a vacation than a job, especially when the big bosses spend more time on the slopes than in the office. As much as she loves her job, Tru wishes she could air out her human resources expertise more often. Her colleagues are happy to skate by, but things start to change when the new CFO arrives. Not everyone is happy about Renske's budget tightening measures. It doesn't help that her stoic demeanor makes them believe she's a cold, unfeeling android. Always willing to think the best of people, Tru sets out to discover if Renske is really as imperturbable as she seems.

"FROZEN'S AT IT AGAIN," Mina complained from her cubicle next to mine after finishing another marathon gossip session on the phone with a friend in finance.

I swallowed an uncharacteristic sigh, tired of Mina forgetting we were supposed to be working and exasperated with my colleagues' constant barrage of negativity, especially concerning Frozen. Also known as Frigid and Arctic and Nippy and Frosty and many other chilly adjectives, Frozen headed our finance department with what most of the employees considered an icy fist. She controls the purse strings for the company, often allowing our CEO to shift responsibility for the difficult decisions onto the CFO's shoulders. Her broad, gorgeous, statuesque shoulders. And by often, I mean always, which makes her the bad guy in the eyes of nearly everyone at headquarters.

"We have to work the holidays. All of us!" Mina whined when I didn't bite at her obvious conversation starter. "Just because she's a Scrooge nobody loves doesn't mean the rest of us don't have family and loved ones we want to spend the holidays with."

"Are you talking about Frozen?"

"Did someone mention Frigid?"

"Ugh, Coldfront is such a drag."

Whenever there was something to complain about, work in my department and the three others sharing our floor came to a stop as if a wrecking ball swung through the office and we couldn't help but gape in shock. Due to the nature of our business, that being a ski resort, slash vacation destination, slash adventure holiday, slash corporate retreat, the atmosphere around here was always casual. Half the people worked here just to get the free season pass to ski each winter. But work did need to get done, especially in the corporate office, and yet these people took any excuse to break from performing their duties. It didn't matter the subject, all of a sudden, they'd drop everything and turn the office into one of those morning shows with five hosts who all talk at once. Frozen was one of their favorite subjects.

"You wouldn't believe the stunt Glacial pulled yesterday."

"What's Polar done now?"

"Who? Frostbite?"

My fingers kept clicking away at the keyboard as I researched benefits options for the upcoming enrollment period while my ears kept being assaulted by my coworkers and their crazy fascination with Frozen. My own fascination differed greatly from theirs, and I'd been very careful to keep that away from my colleagues. With any other beautiful woman traipsing through town or signing on to work a winter season, my colleagues might urge me to give her a try, especially if the guys in the office had all struck out. Not so with Frozen. No one thought of her as human, much less capable of returning affection.

"We all have to take a shift over the holidays," Mina repeated, raking a hand through her midnight black hair and pursing her blood red lips. "On Thanksgiving and Christmas!"

Like those were the only holidays. My eyes rolled, and my mouth issued the held back sigh. I was known for my optimistic personality. Not unrealistically bubbly, just positive and encouraging, and generally cheerful.

"What's wrong, Tru?"

Which was why I keep sighing to a minimum in the company of others. They'd caught me. Though I didn't know how with their loud and unstoppable complaint session carrying on. Still they managed to hear one little sigh, and now I'd need to offer an explanation for the atypical response. I pointed at my screen. "Frustrated with some of these bene selections."

"You're working?"

We were at work where work usually happens. Was this a trick question?

"How can you work when we're talking about Frosty Nero ruining our holidays?"

"Is she really, though?" my mouth spoke before my brain could stop it.

All conversation came to a vacuous standstill. Every pair of eyes cut my way. In my role as a human resources coordinator, I knew every one of these people, helped hire many of them, fought for their benefit options, listened when they had conflicts to resolve, and many other personnel related duties no one else wanted or could figure out how to accomplish. If something needed to get done and their immediate supervisor wasn't open to the idea, I was their next stop. For me to contradict something universally agreed upon just wasn't done. By anyone, most especially someone as useful and reasonable and cordial as me.

"She's declared war on Christmas."

"Oh, please," someone else jumped in. I recognized him for the ardent liberal he was. He'd definitely take offense to applying that particular conservative tagline to someone's actions around here.

"Yeah, don't confuse the whole 'Merry Christmas' versus 'Happy Holidays' thing with Icehouse making us work on the days we should get off."

"She won't let us say Merry Christmas either."

My second sigh turned into a cough to keep from being scrutinized again. There'd been no memo sent around on this topic, and if there had been, she wouldn't have been the one to issue it. She didn't stick her nose into such trivial things, not on a corporate-wide level. She might try reasoning with someone in private, but she wouldn't make it a policy.

Not that I knew her all that well. We'd been in meetings together, been on a few of the same committees, shared a table at lunch once, and a few other chance meetings, but I didn't really know her as anyone other than an absolute professional. I wanted to get to know her, but she scared me a little. She wasn't called Frozen for her similarity to the Disney princess. Her demeanor was reserved at best, downright brusque at worst.

"She's ruining Christmas, Tru."

My snort of laughter was less than gracious, but really? Ruining Christmas? Like she was a medieval queen with the power to cancel Christmas in all the villages of her empire. "Why shouldn't everyone have to work on Thanksgiving and over Hanukah and on Christmas and New Years and Winter Solstice and every other holiday? Why should it be down to those of us without kids or without visiting family or without a spouse or pets or aliens or whatever to surround us on those days and give us an excuse not to work when our workplace is open?"

The hospitality manager looked offended. "You don't know what it's like not being there when your kids are opening presents."

No, I didn't and wouldn't any time soon if I didn't start dating again. This past year hadn't provided a lot of opportunities or time to date, but my dating and potential parenting prospects weren't relevant here. What I did know was how I spent a minimum of nine hours working every holiday because of the preferential treatment shown to married employees.

"Neither do you, Kay," I talked back, also uncharacteristically. "You've had every Christmas off, which is more than I can say for half the people in here. Many of us end up working nine or ten-hour shifts on holidays so we can give parents like you the day off."

"You've never complained before," she huffed, wiping at the hank of strawberry blond hair she could never get to stay behind her ear.

"I try not to complain about work while working because we have great jobs. I love working here, and if I have to work on the holidays to remain employed, I don't see anything wrong with that. With all of us pitching in this year, not only will we avoid the massive pile of complaints we usually receive from visitors on those understaffed days, but we'll be able to cut everyone's shift down to three hours. If you ask me, it's a brilliant plan."

Their expressions varied greatly. All of the singles were nodding their heads and thinking about the benefits of the CFO's plan, while all the married folk looked like they were biting into something bitter. Usually, the CEO made taking holiday shifts voluntary until not enough volunteers stood up. He'd then give a healthy nudge to every single-o on staff, or he'd let the mountain and lodge go grossly understaffed for the day. Invariably the place would be a madhouse within two hours of opening, and the guests would get visibly riled. We'd set a record for bad reviews posted last Christmas. Which is why Frozen's plan to make everyone, not just those who worked on the mountain or in guest services positions, put in a few hours on every holiday was a good one.

"No one ever said they minded getting paid double-time before. It's going too far to make those of us who work in the office take a shift on the mountain. How does my work skill translate to selling tickets and helping people onto the lifts? That's just stupid and a waste of my talent."

Like she had only one work skill. Although, come to think of it...no, that was just mean.

"You could choose to think the only reason you have a job is because people need to buy those tickets and get onto those lifts."

"Wow, tell us how you really feel, Tru," someone snickered in the background.

Oh, if they only knew how I really felt. This place ran more like a high school summer camp than the thriving ski resort business it should be. Rather than embrace the onus for maintaining the economy of the town surrounding us, the resort continued to act as if it was merely an accessory to the ski town. Changing that attitude among the executives had been one of my goals since starting here five years ago. It was a slow shift in the work environment, starting with adjusting the hiring practices from winter ski enthusiasts to dedicated year-round employees in the HQ positions. Still, it took bringing in Frozen, aka Renske Van der Valk, as CFO last June to make the executives recognize the significance of the business to the town and its inhabitants. Things had been changing quickly, not massively, just quickly, and not to everyone's liking, but beneficial to our bottom line.

Then, there was the personal side of how I felt. How my insides would heat and swirl whenever I caught sight of the lovely Ms. Van der Valk. Her stylish wardrobe was eye-catching enough, but it was her enigmatic personality that kept me interested. She wasn't an open book like the rest of my colleagues. Her imperturbable disposition and dislike of holidays seemed to be the only facts most of us knew about her. She wore a professional attitude at all times, and it clearly put people off. They considered her aloof or detached or haughty. They were certain of their judgment. I was certain there was much more to her than her impassive front. Finding out became a bit of a treasure hunt for me.

"Listen," I started in an appeasing tone, "I've been trying for years to get Gus to agree to cross training of guest services and mountain positions so we can pitch in on those days when the roads are impossible to get through for many of us. We all know how to ski, and we all know how to serve customers. It may not be what our job titles are, but selling tickets, renting out equipment, serving coffee, working the lift lines, these are all jobs we can handle for a few hours over a few days every winter. It's not too much to ask, especially if it means I get to go home earlier on Thanksgiving and Christmas this year. I, for one, am grateful she's made this change."

"Frozen."

"Bitter."

"Iceland."

"Glacial."

"Icebox."

"Enough," I said, putting a stop to the volley of synonyms for what they felt was a less than friendly person. On the third eyeroll of the day, I caught sight of Renske Van der Valk standing on the landing for our floor. She turned back toward the open steel and timber staircase, abandoning her plan to seek out someone for a meeting after hearing every one of the unkind nicknames tossed out.

My heart sank as I watched the tall, lean form move to climb back up the stairs. Her short blond—admittedly icy-blond—hair carried the characteristic mussiness I'd come to recognize not as deliberate, but rather the hasty result of a lone styling in the morning and maintained by hand swipes throughout the day even if the wind attacked while she visited other buildings on the resort and village grounds. No one had ever caught her spending time studying herself in the ladies' washroom. Styling and touchups didn't interest her. She made sure she was put together every morning, but once she reached work, she didn't bother with upkeep. Several times I'd spy her walking to her car, her face slightly shiny and her hair a bit lopsided from the finger rakes through one side more than the other. Today, she looked as lovely as ever, not billboard ready or big screen gorgeous or even prom queen beautiful. Her attractiveness stemmed from the beauty that is ordinary. Nothing on her face made people fixate like with other gorgeous women. Renske's face had features that were unremarkable. Together they worked beautifully, but without a standout, she'd never be considered anything more than attractive and only to those of us who measured beauty among commonplace things.

Before climbing out of sight, her head turned, amber eyes locking with mine. The knot in my stomach plummeted as heat scorched my face. She'd caught me staring. How humiliating. We'd been gossiping about her, it kept her from coming onto the floor, and now she knew someone was staring at her, possibly knew someone was checking her out. *Way to be a stalker, Tru.*

Then, for the briefest of moments, a twinkle brightened her gaze, and the dread and heat and embarrassment I was experiencing disappeared in an instant. She'd heard the unflattering nicknames and seen my blatant perusal, and she was amused. Possibly amusingly annoyed, but definitely not angry.

2 | TRU

AROUND THE TABLE SAT
every department executive and me, not a department
executive. My boss needed my help to catch her up after
taking a sabbatical for the entire offseason. What would
that be like? Ditch the job for five months and not starve to
death or lose the house or cut back on everyday expenses?
Just one more advantage to having a partner, someone to
fall back on, someone to support your choices and
existence, someone concerned with your mental health. It
had done her a lot of good, stepping away like that. She'd
been headed for burnout, but the break helped reassert her
passion for the job. Although, passion may be a strong word
for it. She'd never really been gung-ho for the job.

"Are you going to be able to smooth things over, Carly?"
Gus asked my boss.

She promptly turned to me, not knowing what the CEO
was talking about. I assumed he was talking about the new
holiday work schedule, but he could be talking about

something else. Gus tended to talk in generalities. His often-distracted personality didn't pin itself to one topic. For instance, we'd just been debating raising lift ticket prices for the season. He could be talking about placating the locals, but that question should go to the marketing director.

"The rate hike or the holiday schedule?" I asked to clarify.

He stroked his billowy, silver beard, a signal he couldn't remember what he'd asked. Seconds passed before it came to him. "Both, actually."

The marketing director had checked out as usual, so I looked at Carly to see if she wanted me to tackle this. She lifted the shoulder closest to me in a shrug. "We could offer discounted lift tickets at the market for the locals so they don't think we're gouging them." I checked with Renske since she recommended the lift ticket price hike. My suggestion might give the impression of disagreeing with her.

Her eyes bounced my way, interest making them sparkle. Mid-morning, her hair still looked perfectly put together, product keeping the longer front layers swooped up off her forehead and back to lay mid-scalp, met by the tapered close cut down to her natural hairline. The mussiness was fun to spot, but this refined look always drew my gaze.

"As long as we sell them in packets, not just one at a time, the discount will be offset by the volume," she confirmed. "Locals aren't our target market when it comes to boosting revenues."

"Great idea, Tru," Gus complimented, his eyes darting to the marketing director who should have had the same idea. "Good thinking, Valk," he said to Renske. For some reason, he always called her Valk, as if her full last name was too much to handle and her first name insignificant, or more likely for him, unpronounceable.

"We could get the concierges at the hotels to sell them as well," the marketing director finally checked back into the meeting.

"We make our money on tourists. They come here to ski. Giving them a discount to ski won't entice more skiing, it'll just lower our gate." Renske's tone wasn't sarcastic or condescending, but the looks she got from my boss and the marketing director said they took offense. Logic ruled her response, something they should already know, but they'd hold it against her for making one of them look like he didn't know his job.

"Makes sense," Aiden said as he seemed to snap out of the eyes-wide-open nap he'd been taking. Any other COO would have been alert and possibly even driving the meeting, but Gus and Aiden never adhered to corporate norms. "How's the seasonal hiring going?"

My eyes flicked to the CEO to see if he wanted to tackle his other question first, but alas, his ADD kept him from following through. "We've still got several positions to fill. The seasonal workers are just starting to hit town. I've got calls out to more than half from last year to check if they'll be returning."

"Why not all?" The marketing director clearly wanted to contradict something.

"We had some issues with several of them last year," my boss answered.

"We need more thorough training," Aiden suggested, effectively tripling his usual input at these meetings.

"My department does its best with the limited time we have between their arrival in town and opening day." Carly sounded defensive, even if it was spot on. We gave them a few days of training and hoped they picked up the rest from our regulars on the job. It was the best we could do without paying them year-round to keep them in town and consistently trained for the winter busy season.

"Shadows," Renske said. Every eye turned to her. "Make them shadow your regulars for a half day every week in the beginning. Call it a refresher morning or whatever to soothe their egos, but make sure they understand their way is not the only way to perform their jobs."

"I like it, Valk." Gus nodded. "Can you put that into action, Carly?"

Her gaze shot to me and a knot formed in my stomach. One more duty to add to the list. Adjust the personnel manual, change some training slides, and implement the new training procedure. Yay, more work.

"Once the HQ staff is completely trained up on all the guest services positions, everyone can help out with the shadowing duties." Renske spoke directly to me, having interpreted Carly's look for the extra work it imposed on me.

"Yeah, what about that?" Gus circled back to his original question.

"The holiday schedule?" Carly clarified and looked at me again. As nice as it had been not having a boss breathing over my shoulder all summer, her sabbatical was proving disruptive to our department now that she was back.

I looked at Renske. "It's a good idea, both to get everyone trained up and to alleviate the burden of the holidays falling on a small group of employees."

"I don't know about burden," Gus hemmed and then looked guilty when he realized I was one of the burdened ones every holiday.

"Of course, it's a burden," Renske spoke up, obviously not recognizing Gus's contriteness, or choosing to ignore it. "You've got a dozen or so employees who work every hour of every holiday and a handful of others who work part-time shifts. You can't keep asking these employees to carry the full load of fifty others."

"Holidays are special, always have been," the marketing director said.

"Holidays are just like any other day if your workplace is open. It may be slower, it may have happier customers, but it's just another workday for your employees. You've been paying triple time for four hours to those employees who cover twelve-hour shifts, and there still aren't enough employees to satisfy the needs of every guest on the mountain. It's time you stopped treating the holidays like they're anything but another day."

Scoffs sounded around the conference table. When you live in a winter wonderland like ours, the winter holidays do tend to make everyone feel as if they live in a Hallmark Holiday movie. The holiday spirit captures everyone. Except Renske, evidently.

"I don't know if we need to go that far," Gus said. "But you're right. It shouldn't fall to a small group to keep us open on Thanksgiving and Christmas." He turned to Carly. "Work up a preliminary shift schedule, and I'll take a look."

Carly didn't bother glancing at me this time. She didn't have to. Everyone in the room knew I'd be the one working up the schedule. Mina would have to finalize the research on the insurance options on her own. She'd be just as thrilled about that as I was to be re-tasked with this.

"That's it for today," Gus called a close to the meeting, not checking to see if anyone else had other issues to bring up. He needed to find something to satisfy his distraction. He'd likely be mountain biking down one of the offseason trails of the lower bowl very soon.

Most everyone got up with him as he jumped from his seat and swept out of the room. The COO and marketing director made their way out together. Carly and the heads of guest services, mountain ops, and hotel management huddled together at one end of the table. I gathered my tablet and stood only to find Renske's eyes fastened on me.

The intense scrutiny wobbled my knees, and I had to set a hand on the table to steady my stance.

"What's the big deal about holidays?" she asked in a bewildered tone that clearly confirmed she hadn't noticed our town could be used as a movie set for every Hallmark Christmas movie ever made.

I wasn't entirely sure she was speaking to me. This was the first personal question, well, personalish question, she'd ever asked me. Ever asked anyone at work, as far as I knew.

"I get that people have family obligations," she continued. "But everyone acts like it's some magical wormhole they get to slip into for the day."

Wormhole? I wanted to laugh, but she probably wasn't kidding. Some of my colleagues thought she might have Asperger's. They needed a label to explain her standoffish and overly logical behavior. It didn't matter that they only knew her at work where professionalism should explain her mannerisms. It also bothered me when people thought any deviation from the social norms needed a "condition" to explain the deviation.

"They get the same number of days off as anyone else in the workforce; they're just not according to some holiday schedule." The slight wrinkle in her forehead indicated how this twisted in her mind. Perhaps she had an anti-religious opposition to the holidays or objected to their commercialization. Or it could be as simple as she stated.

The holidays were nothing more than another day on the calendar to her.

"Well, I, for one, am thankful you suggested the change." I smiled and her eyes dropped to my now visible dimples. Her preoccupation made my heart thump, especially when she needed to turn her head to break her gaze.

She swiveled in her seat, following the turn of her head. Her eyes swept the room, confirming we were now alone. "Even though you're stuck working out the schedule and having to listen to everyone complain about it?"

"I can handle venting."

Her amber gaze came back and strolled over me, pondering my response. "You shouldn't have to, Ms. Daring."

My voice caught in my throat as she stood from the table. How could the sound of my name from her lips make my mouth dry up? It was just a name. She'd used it before, but I didn't remember it affecting me so much. Had my appreciation for her attractiveness developed into a full-fledged crush? Considering how standoffish she was, this spelled trouble for me. It was one thing to admire her from afar, quite another to experience real feelings for her. Our encounters were getting more frequent, and still, they lacked basic familiarity. She was a far cry from the iceberg my colleagues considered her to be, but she continued to maintain a professional distance.

"It's Tru," I managed as she glided through the doorway.

On her way out, she looked back, mouth twitching into a small smile. "It is."

I felt my lips tug in response, heart pounding again. Her play on words managed to narrow the professional distance she cloaked herself with better than any in-depth conversation could. Next time we were alone together, I'd see what I could do to strip away that cloak.

3 | TRU

THE FRONT DOOR OPENED and closed noisily, followed by a cheery, "Hi, Tru! What's for dinner?"

A smile split my face as it always did whenever my sister joined me. Ten years my junior, she and I have always been close. Sure, there were times in my teen years when it was a drag to have to babysit instead of going out with friends, but our parents made sure those gigs were only occasional. My friends all babysat nightmare kids for extra cash. I was lucky with my sister.

She bounded into the kitchen, a similar smile on her beautiful face. Her thick glasses tilted on her wide nose, probably from whipping off her knit hat as she came inside. She was too excited to bother adjusting them before finding me. Her enthusiasm buoyed any mood I might ever be in.

"Hiya, Blythe. How was your day?" My fingers reached out and tweaked the arm of her glasses to tuck back into place. The plastic frames righted on her face, giving a clear view of hazel eyes beyond the lenses. With one last adjustment, her light brown hair resettled into her usual chin-length bob.

She stepped close to wrap her arms around me. This was a typical greeting. She was a champion hugger. Didn't matter how bad the day, one of her hugs would set anyone to rights. My arms squeezed her tight, something that used to calm her as a child still helped her as an adult. What hadn't been typical was the slight shrug she gave before hugging me hello.

"Did anything happen?" I was overprotective. I knew this. My sister knew this. She didn't always like it, thought it meant I didn't see her as the adult she now was. Our circumstances, our age difference, our family dynamic all contributed to this overprotectiveness. She mostly saw it as a display of love and defended me just as fervently.

"My boss is a jerk."

That was as harsh as she ever got. She saw the good in everyone, even her jerk of a supervisor. As optimistic as I was, I had a hard time seeing the good in him. Thankfully, he didn't work with her, just assigned her tasks and let her work, but he wasn't a pleasant guy. If he worked at the resort, my colleagues would never stop complaining about him.

Many times, I'd thought about encouraging her to look for a different job, but she liked routine. Needed it, and without a college degree, her choices were limited to similarly structured jobs with likely the same kind of insecure bosses.

"Did you kick him in the shins?" I pulled back and grinned at her.

She pushed at my shoulders, returning my grin. Her round face didn't have the dimples mine did, but her smile was no less potent. How anyone could turn away from her as they often did, I'd never know. Different scared people. We learned that from the moment she was born. It didn't matter how sweet she was, how loving. What people saw was the chubby flat face, small slanted eyes, thick glasses, short neck, and a few other physical characteristics typical of Down's Syndrome. They saw the syndrome, not the beautiful girl, and it made my heart ache every time. Her boss saw her that way, and I wanted to shake him whenever I stopped by to pick her up.

"He's such a smarty pants. Doesn't think I can do my job without telling me what to do every day. The job never changes, and he still thinks I need instructions."

I ran my hand over her back in soothing circles. "He probably got yelled at by his boss for being an idiot and wanted to take it out on someone. You can't let it get to you."

"I know," she said, but it was a reflex response, something she used to give her the extra time she needed to work through things.

"He'll move onto something else tomorrow like he always does. You're good at your job, just remember that."

"I know," she repeated and settled against my side, looking down at the pans I had on the stove. "What's for dinner?"

"Are you staying? No date tonight?" I teased, but my heart twisted at the notion. She'd only moved out a year ago and into a shared apartment arranged by Social Services. She had three other roommates, two with Down's and one with autism. They were all the best of friends, but recently, Blythe and Sonny had started dating. It pained me to think about my little sister dating and eventually having sex, or already having sex—no, la-la-la, don't want to think about it. She's my little sister, and she deserves happiness. I could be an adult about that. She probably didn't want to think about me having sex either. It had been so long, I could hardly think about it myself.

Renske's face popped into my mind. Okay, now I could think about me having sex. Hot, steamy, writhing sex with that statuesque beauty.

"Mmm, chicken and rice casserole? Did you know I was coming by? You're making my favorite."

I loved her enthusiasm. She enjoyed food and had been so gracious about my steep learning curve when it came to cooking. After four years, I could now hold my own, maybe even against some professional chefs. Through my twenties, I'd subsisted on salads and grilling or going out to eat, but with our parents' death, I had to take on many roles, including household cook. Balanced meals were a must to help with Blythe's iron deficiency and thyroid issues, and they certainly didn't hurt me. Once I hit thirty, my metabolism couldn't have kept up with my former eating habits anyway.

"One of your favorites," I reminded her because she had so many favorites. She didn't understand why people limited themselves to one favorite something. She had multiple favorites of everything. She loved and loved and loved. It was her best quality. Not that she didn't get frustrated or angry, but we'd been raised not to let things drag us down. Bright sides could be found around every corner.

"Top five favorite." She took over stirring the rice as I turned to the chicken browning in another pan.

"How's Sonny?"

"Dreamy," she sighed.

Dreamy? She could make me laugh any time, any day. "What's he doing for dinner?"

"At his parents."

Sonny had gone to a rival high school two towns over, but they'd met at a summer camp before her last year in high school. They'd been friends ever since, and once she expressed interest in living on her own, we coordinated through her social worker a home for a few other young adults ready to try living on their own. I was thrilled Sonny and Jolie were willing to relocate so they could all share with Blythe and another boy who lived in town. I didn't know Gideon as well as I knew Sonny and Jolie. He wasn't as open as they were and wary of new people. I liked him and knew he was good for the other kids, just like they were good for him. They taught him that being around people was nothing to fear, and he taught them that being cautious around people wasn't a bad thing. It was still hard to think of her living on her own, though. At twenty-three, she was just like every other woman her age, wanting independence and friends and fun and love, but she was also unique and still naïve about so many things. It worried me, kept me up some nights, but then I'd spend one afternoon or evening with her and all the worry would wash away.

"Did you have fun at work today?" She believed everyone should have fun at work. She did, whenever her boss wasn't exerting what little authority he actually had.

"Guess what?" I tipped the partially cooked chicken into a baking dish and watched as Blythe poured the creamy rice in. I slapped a cover on the dish and shoved it into the oven.

"What?" Blythe bounced up onto to her toes because she loved the "guess what?" game.

"It has to do with the holidays."

"You're going to make tacos for Thanksgiving instead of turkey?"

"Is that what you want?"

"No!" she screeched, gripping my arms for emphasis. "Are you flying us to Hawaii?"

"Is that where you want to spend the holidays? No snow and in a hotel?"

"No!" she called out again, giggling now. "Okay, what?"

"I only have to work a few hours on holidays this season."

"How many hours?"

"Three at most."

"Then you can be home?"

"Yep."

"For the whole day and night?"

"All but three hours. Do you want to babysit the turkey while I'm working or should I go in after we've eaten?" As the schedule maker for the shifts, I could decide which shift worked best for me before deciding everyone else's fate.

"Oh, I thought maybe I might try cooking this year. Sonny wants to come over if that's okay. His parents eat in the afternoon, so maybe you could help me put the turkey in before you go to work, and then when you get back, we can eat at dinnertime."

I blinked, surprised by the request. She loved my cooking, loved the holiday feasts we tried so very hard to make just like when Mom and Dad were alive. For her to want to change that was a big deal. "Sure, honey. That sounds like a great idea."

"I know." She grinned her big beautiful grin. "You should invite someone this year. You always let me invite people. It's your turn to bring someone."

My mind cycled through my friends and friendly coworkers. Any of them would say yes if they were free, but the only one I really wanted at my table was Renske, which said way too much about me and the no longer refutable crush I had on her.

4 | TRU

HOUR THREE OF OUR
customer service training session, and I could tell we would
have constant problems with five of the twelve in the group.
These twelve would be working in various positions in the
ski lodge, which meant they'd have prolonged contact with
our guests. The problem five hoped they'd be working on
the slopes, but mountain positions were coveted and held
by the seasonals with longevity. Even with two more
intensive training days, I likely wouldn't be able to reset
their expectations.

"You could get a high schooler to bus tables," one of
them protested.

"I could if they were available all day, but being high
schoolers, they're in school. Plus, busing tables is only part
of your job." If she gets it, that is. She hadn't read anything
into the tone I used whenever any of them asked stupid
questions or made entitled comments. She thought the job
was hers because she'd been placed in training. She chose

to ignore the part about making it through training first. "Kitchen staff have a variety of duties, one of which is to clear and clean the tables in the dining and sitting areas."

"I'd rather sell tickets."

"You'll be training for all lodge positions. Variety keeps it interesting."

"Does that mean we'll get to be on ski patrol or groom the slopes or anything that involves boarding?"

"First Years work the lodge or the grounds or the parking lots."

Groans sounded from every direction. As much as I loved my sister, sometimes I wondered about her generation. These youngsters showed up every year thinking they'd spend six of their eight-hour shift boarding on the mountain. They applied to positions that specifically listed their duties and where they'd take place, but they chose to ignore that posting and ask for what they wanted.

"That's lunch, everyone," I told them before letting sarcasm taint their already poor impression of the job so far. "See you back in a half hour."

"A half hour? How are we supposed to get into town, eat lunch, and get back in a half hour?" a thus far quiet person spoke up.

"You're not. Bring a lunch or buy it from the lodge or one of the cafés in the village."

"We'll go broke doing that."

"Not if you pack a lunch." My parting shot brought on more grumbling, but they all scrambled to get to the door before they lost any more of their lunch break.

Mina pushed through the departing trainees, eyes sparkling. "I got Thanksgiving off. That'll show Frozen."

My eyes would roll out of their sockets soon if my coworkers didn't stop complaining about things not worthy of complaint. "Show her what? That you know how to put in for a floating holiday? Not everyone is needed that day. Some of you are bound to get the day off."

"Yeah, well, she shouldn't be telling people when they have to work. She's a numbers geek."

I shook my head, unable to stop myself from contradicting her. This fascination with Renske was overriding my usual inclination to avoid conflict. "She's not telling people when to work. She looked at our holiday payroll figures and suggested ways to bring them back within normal range. It's a good policy. If you want to use your floating holidays on the actual holidays, go for it."

"Sounds like you're all fangirl for her."

"Give her a break, Mina. She's here to watch over the finances, and she's doing a good job of it. Remember last year, Gus was considering layoffs because he couldn't keep up with payroll? How we had to wait three weeks to get our paychecks? Now Gus is back to his usual spending habits and hiring more people." More than necessary, in my opinion. Four people were now doing what two people used to accomplish, which according to Gus, meant we also needed more managers to manage those extra people. "Obviously, Renske is getting a handle on the expenses and coming up with ways to increase revenues if he's no longer talking about layoffs."

"Big time fangirl," she kidded, winking a dark blue eye at me.

"Shuddup." I waved her out of the training room and grabbed my bag to head over to the lodge.

Our office, a three-level building with a chalet style façade, stood next to the grand ski lodge with its open architecture of round logs, stacked stone, and oversized windows. A covered walkway connected the buildings and started up on the other side to extend to the sprawling, European-inspired, two-story inn. The ski village with its shops and cafés nestled within walking distance of the inn. The mountain, with its beautifully chiseled streaks of white snowy runs and dark trees in the winter, or rugged swathes of brown earth and massive evergreen trees in the summer, served as the backdrop to every view one could have while on the resort grounds. Having grown up here, I should be tired of the view. Instead, I paused on the walkway outside to take it in. A bitter edge to the wind put an end to warm weather activities last week. Soon enough, snow would shroud the mountain, and skiers and snowboarders from all over would swarm the area.

Inside the lodge, I walked past the employee locker room through a security door to the public areas. Directly across the main lobby off the side entrance closest to the inn were the retail and equipment rental shops. A four-sided coffee shop in the lobby forced all guests to succumb to their caffeine habit or file around it to get to the leisure area of the lodge. Thirty-foot ceilings with wall to wall windows showcasing the slopes beyond made the space feel larger than it was. Club chairs and sofas clustered around a massive fireplace for guests who wanted a break from skiing. Shared tables and pub tabletops filled the dining area. Our cafeteria had evolved into a mini food court with multiple food counters in every culinary preference. Remodeled the summer before last, the space finally had an efficient design which funneled people in, through, and out to the cashiers quickly.

"Yo, Tru." One of the payroll clerks raised a hand in greeting. He was sitting among four other HQ staff, lingering over their lunch break, which should have ended five minutes ago.

"Hey, Phil, guys." I took a seat and opened my insulated lunch bag. Bringing a lunch was the only option for most of the staff. The cafeteria prices weren't quite at amusement park levels, but close enough.

"Get this, Tru." Phil leaned across the empty chair between us. "O'Keefe tried it on with Icebox."

"And got rejected!" one of the finance guys taunted.

"Spanked on his ass rejected," a marketing guy added.

"Screw you," O'Keefe mumbled. "I never would have gone for it if you guys hadn't bet me. She's a total ice queen bitch."

"Because she wouldn't go out with you?" I couldn't help being drawn into this conversation.

"Because she looked at me with those cold eyes of hers, no smile, no expression, just nothing."

"She didn't respond?" I prompted, curious now as to how she acted when a direct personal question was posed.

"Well." His eyes shot to his buddies. He was a good-looking guy, wavy hair to his collar, perpetual five o'clock shadow, baby blue eyes, and age appropriate. Nothing overtly apparent to hold her back if she'd been open to dating. Nothing other than a particular type she might go for. Or a particular gender. "I asked if she wanted to grab a drink with me, casual like, and she said she didn't want to."

"What did she say exactly that makes her such an ice queen bitch?" I was getting sick of these qualifications, and despite my department's many lectures on what makes for a hostile environment in the workplace, nothing seemed to take. They saw this as freedom of speech on their lunch break. No supervisors were around. They were all pals, and the object of their distaste was nowhere to be seen. Who could possibly take offense?

"She said no, all right?"

"That's it? You said, 'Would you like to get a drink, Renske?' and she said, 'No.' That's what makes her a bitch?"

"She's a block of ice, Tru, you can't deny that," Phil defended his friend.

"Wait, that's how you say her name?" finance guy asked, a frown scrunching his brow.

"Maybe that's why she rejected me."

"Because you didn't pronounce her name correctly?" I was straying from my usual chipper demeanor again but didn't care. "I doubt it. I also bet she added a 'thank you' to the end of her rejection."

His gaze darted away. Yep, caught him. She'd politely declined his offer without correcting the mispronunciation of her name, and he still thought she was an ice queen bitch. It was time for another all-staff meeting about acceptable attitudes and treatment of colleagues in the workplace.

"Dude, she acted like you were offering to get her a cup of coffee, not take her on a date. Total burn."

"Face plant, yo," Phil needled him. "You had to try, though. She's got to be wild in bed. All those controlled, cold types are."

"That's going too far." I knocked my fist on the tabletop. "I'm putting my HR hat on here. You guys need to quit this kind of talk in the workplace."

"We're just joking, Tru."

"Joke offsite, and your lunch break is up."

"Somebody's wound tight." Phil turned his needlepoint to me. He was indiscriminate with the needling, which somehow made him liked by all. "Come out with us this weekend, Tru. Some pretty tourist can help you loosen up."

"Just an offer to go out, personal time, offsite, no biggie," finance guy kidded, then noticed my elaborate show of looking at my watch. They all took the hint and gathered up their containers and bags to get back over to the office.

The nature of our business made for a casual atmosphere on the grounds and in the office. Chatter like this went unimpeded and unrecognized as inappropriate. Renske was the first entirely professional employee most of them had ever worked with, and they didn't know how to handle it.

As if conjured by thought, Renske strode past the four-sided fireplace, her mouth upturned and head nodding at the guests settled around the fire for a relaxing afternoon instead of the hiking or biking or ATV riding they'd planned before the weather dropped twenty degrees to the mid-thirties in one day. She was always "on" in front of the guests, and in front of employees, come to think. She treated tourists and locals who visited the resort as if they were her houseguests, no matter the inconvenience to her day. I admired that about her. Guest services never suited me. I could be welcoming in short bursts, but I was happy for my job in HR. She looked like she wouldn't mind transitioning out of finance into customer service.

She stopped and answered a few questions for a cluster of women already two sheets to the wind at one in the afternoon. Her six-foot frame towered over the seated women, her polished attire looked out of place compared to their tight jeans and cashmere sweaters, and her refined short hairstyle contrasted greatly with their fluffy hair sprayed locks.

My eyes followed her every move. She was so together, so collected, so professional. Was I as crass as my colleagues with my desire to find a crack in her perfectly controlled persona? Just a tiny fissure, something that would allow a glimpse of the glowy warmth she hid from everyone. I knew it was there. I wasn't sure how I knew, I just did.

"Hello, Ms. Daring," her voice floated down to me.

"Ms. Van der Valk." I smiled up at her. At five-nine, I didn't often need to look up to women, but I could get used to it with her. "Lunch break?"

"Getting a cappuccino."

What did she eat for lunch? The one time we'd shared a table, she was finishing a pear, the rest of her lunch already eaten. Was she a healthy eater? Did she watch what she ate? Was there someone at home who worried about that? Worried about her and cared for her? Without Blythe to care for and care about me, I'd be lost. My life would be so empty. I didn't want that for anyone, especially Renske.

"Did you take a lunch break today, Renske?"

She seemed to settle back on her heels. "I don't believe you've ever used my name before."

My mouth dried up again. Just one sentence, and she could make my nerves jump. "We've always kept to titles, seems everyone does with you. Is that what you prefer?"

Her brow spiked up. "Only with people who can't get my name right." She smiled, full and lovely for the first time, and the desert in my mouth spread through the rest of my body. If she touched me, I'd disintegrate. "Enjoy the rest of your day, Tru."

How could I not?

5 | TRU

SNOWFLAKES THE SIZE OF quarters fell from the sky blanketing the grounds. First snow of the season. The forecast called for flurries all week, which was great news for the mountain. We might be able to move up our planned opening for the ski season. Even one extra week made a huge difference to our profit margin.

My interviewee slumped back against her chair. Nothing about her said she could handle the mix of personalities and temperaments she'd see as a ski instructor. She must have thought she'd be giving private lessons to rich women she could gossip with or rich men she could flirt with all day. Even if those wealthy yet lonely and gullible people signed up for lessons, she wouldn't be the one instructing them. Only experienced ski instructors gave private lessons.

"Like, I've been skiing since I was sixteen." Her tone suggested I should have known that already. "I know what I'm doing."

I've been skiing since I was five; it didn't make me able to teach groups of tourists with little to no skiing or boarding experience. It didn't even qualify me to deal one-on-one with rich flirt-worthy women.

"How would you handle a group with two small kids who've never been on skis before and three teenagers who take off down the hill before learning how to stop?"

"Like, that's gonna happen."

"That will happen. Beginner groups are a mix of complete newbies and people who've been on skis or boards a few times. We try to keep their skill level and ages similar, but sometimes, you'll get a mix. You'll need to have a plan to keep everyone focused and learning."

"That would suck."

I blinked and then laughed, had to. How could she think that was an appropriate answer to any question in a job interview? She started laughing with me, thinking I'd found her response funny rather than absurd. This was somehow the caliber of candidate our recruiting efforts provided. First thing tomorrow morning, I'd review our listings and where we were posting. Carly usually made those decisions, but something would have to change if this young woman was the result.

"Thanks, we'll let you know." I stood and walked her to the door.

Bringing in the last candidate of the day, I could already tell he would be a better fit. My experience in human resources has given me a lot of insight into finding good employees. Little things such as how dismissive they are when checking in with the receptionist, eye contact when shaking hands, and how quickly they walked said as much as their responses during an interview. If a person isn't friendly with the receptionist, she or he would never be a good candidate to work in guest services. Not maintaining eye contact in a greeting usually indicates the person is hiding something. And dragging heels or leisurely walking is subconscious body language for someone who doesn't really want the job.

I glanced at his application once we'd taken our seats. "You're taking a semester off?"

"The year." He sat up straighter and gave me a sheepish grin. "Sometimes parents don't like hearing you're not college material."

Did that mean once they figured out he was no longer at school, they'd yank his ass off the mountain and back home?

"They know I'm here," he said, reading my mind. "They're all for me getting a job. They think if I have to work eight hours a day every day, I'll get sick of it and go running back to college. They don't understand how anyone would prefer working to college. But I love skiing and I've had full-time summer jobs, and both are better than college."

"You worked at Big Sky part-time in high school?"

"On the weekends, ski instructing. I took the beginners mostly, kids whose parents really needed a two-hour break."

"I know the type. We try to discourage the drive-by dump here."

He laughed and waved a hand. "Actually, most of my kids paid better attention if their parents aren't soccer dads shouting from the sidelines."

What a massive difference from the woman I interviewed before. He was experienced and liked working with kids. The team lead would be thrilled. Very few of her instructors could handle more than one kiddie group a day. This guy sounded like he preferred them.

I stood and shook his hand. "I'm going to walk you over to the team lead. If we catch her before she leaves for the day, she'll want to talk to you."

His eyes sparkled. I was essentially telling him he had the job, which wasn't my decision alone. I shouldn't be promising it before checking his references, but I had a good feeling about him. The team leads and department heads relied on my opinion as much as their own. For the ones who disliked the hiring process, they relied on my opinion more than their own.

We caught the team lead as she was putting on her coat to leave for the day. One look at my smile and she shed the parka, gesturing for my interviewee to sit. I gave them a wave and headed back upstairs to my office.

"Don't know, dude. Just some weird chick hanging out up there." Justin from the web team was saying as he and Lyle from IT pounded down the stairs. Both ignored me as they swept past.

"And you're running scared?"

"You had to be there." They were recent graduates from college. This being their first real job, they preferred their computer screens to socializing with coworkers. And now it seemed, women scared them most of all.

As I neared the landing of the second floor, I could hear a woman's voice ask, "Hello, may I help you?"

Renske's voice. A sparkler went off in my midsection. Maybe I'd catch her before whatever meeting she was heading into. Maybe she was here to meet with me. I'd gladly postpone my departure for a meeting with her.

The response to her inquiry was too soft to hear. I was caught between wanting to skip up the remaining stairs and lingering to hear more of her voice and sigh and swoon a little longer.

"I think she might still be over in the lodge. Is she expecting you?" Renske asked.

"It's first snow."

My sister. Of course. It was first snow. We always have hot chocolate and pie at our favorite bakery in town on the first day of snow. I hadn't forgotten, but I usually swing by her office to pick her up. She mostly traveled by bus, and without the ski shuttle running yet, she would have had to make a transfer to get up here.

"Do you have a tradition on first snow?" Renske asked in the same polite tone she used when speaking with all guests. Not the kind of tone most people used when speaking with my sister. Like she was a small child who couldn't possibly understand anything complex and thus required nothing more than simple repetition of what she says. Most people would have heard my sister's cryptic reply about first snow, and responded with a condescending, "It sure is, sweetie."

"We go out for hot chocolate and pie and sit on the patio and let it snow on us."

I reached the landing and saw my beautiful sister standing close to my beautiful colleague, staring up and up and up at her from her much shorter stature. An inch and a half over five feet, my sister didn't bother with stepping back to better her viewing angle. She found someone interesting to talk to. She'd want to get close to talk.

"Sounds delicious."

"It's the best. You're really tall." Blythe gave an embarrassed laugh. "I mean, I'm short. What's your name? I'm Blythe."

My sister babbles when she gets nervous. I rushed forward to let her know I was there and give her some confidence, but I should have known not to worry with Renske.

"You're not short. You're barely off the average." Renske's hand patted my sister's shoulder as if sensing she needed to be reassured she hadn't said something stupid. "It's nice to meet you, Blythe, I'm Renske."

"Ooo, that's a new name."

"Hi, Blythe," I called out as I neared.

"Tru! It's first snow!" She came forward for a hug.

I squeezed her hello and leaned back. "I thought I'd come get you."

"There was nothing left for me to do today, so he let me go early."

"Well, that's a nice change." A little disturbing, too, but it could be his laziness rearing its head, instead of him trying to make her work dry up for the excuse to lay her off. Her fast food job ended like that. She'd take it hard if it happened again.

"I met Renske." She turned and looked back at her with a big smile.

"She's our chief financial officer." And the frequent occupier of my distracted thoughts. My productivity had dropped slightly since indulging in daydreams I used to be able to quash pretty quickly. Compared to the amount of time most of my colleagues spent on their social media accounts, my brief daydreams shouldn't make me feel guilty about postponing any work.

"A queen of numbers?" Blythe looked to me for confirmation. We talked about all the jobs I helped fill, and she liked to retitle them as queens or kings of whatever they did.

A laugh sounded, and for a moment, I had to look around because it was so unfamiliar. Renske's laugh. As beautiful as she was. "I like the sound of that. We should change my title, Tru."

Blythe joined her laughter. "Tru can do that. She can do anything."

Renske's eyes roamed over me. Not an entirely professional roam, but this wasn't an entirely professional situation. "I bet she can."

"You should come with us for first snow hot chocolate."

Renske grimaced, regret clear on her expression. "I'm stuck finishing some reports, but thank you for the invitation."

"Oh." Blythe's eyes flicked nervously to mine. Sometimes her confidence failed her in social situations. I assured her it happened to everyone, not just her, even if she felt like it at the time. It didn't always lessen the embarrassment when she thought she'd made a social gaffe, though.

"Next time? If it's okay with your sister, too." Renske asked, and gave me a wink that set off even more sparklers in my belly.

"Yes!" Blythe exclaimed, making us laugh with her enthusiasm. "This is the best day. Making new friends is my favorite thing to do."

"Okay, bestie, time to chug some hot chocolate." I squeezed her shoulder.

"I know, let's go." She turned to Renske, and I could feel the stiffness as she held herself back from wanting to hug Renske goodbye. "Have fun with your numbers."

Renske nodded once, amusement dancing in her eyes again. "I always do. Bye for now."

"She's pretty," Blythe said as we hit the staircase.

My head snapped around to check if Renske was still in hearing distance. Thankfully, she was at the marketing director's office door, too far away to hear my sister's matchmaking attempt. She glanced back, catching my stare. I really had to stop doing that. And I would, if she'd stop smiling every time she caught me. I faced forward and started down the stairs.

"It's first snow, be happy with that."

"I am." Blythe linked arms with me. "We should get a whole pie and take the rest home."

We should. Always go for the whole pie instead of a slice. Words to live by.

ICE SCRAPED against my skis as I zigged into a turn near the boundary of my favorite run. Wind blew snowflakes into my goggles, visibility getting more clouded by the turn. I should have waited for the weekend to get in my first run of the season, but after the day I'd had, I couldn't pass up the chance.

My skis glided over the packed snow, thighs jouncing against the uneven terrain. The snow wasn't perfect, a mix of natural and machine made. A week and a half into the season, better snow and conditions were coming soon. I could have waited. Should have waited, but the run called to me. My office had a view of this run. I hadn't asked for it. It just worked out that way. Like a lot of things about this job.

As I neared the lower half of the run, more figures dotted the landscape. The inn was only half full this early in the season, but the rental office was pulling in good numbers already. If the snow was good this year and Gus kept to the frugal spending plan, the company should start making a profit again. Maybe even pay down some of the debt accumulated over the last two years for repairs and remodeling.

A flash of blue came into my periphery, causing me to zag back toward the boundary. If we'd gotten fresh powder, I would have let my skis carry me into the forest lining the run. My preferred skiing conditions excluded crowds. Too many people cluttered the purity of skiing.

Several tourists had stopped in the middle of the lower bowl to take selfies. They'd spent hundreds of dollars on their tickets, equipment rentals, brand new snowsuits, goggles, and helmets. Naturally, that deserved a selfie to commemorate. Not of the scenery or with their friends, no. A selfie wasn't a selfie unless it featured themselves, their new outfits, and silly faces. On their own.

People. They make no sense.

Still, it was a nice place. Not nearly as many visitors here as in my last two postings. The town was a nice size, too, not just a vacation destination. Logging, mining, and the railroad beefed up the town before the ski company existed. Competition could be found within a couple of hours in every direction, including across state lines in Idaho and Wyoming. Having worked for three of the top ski resorts in the country, I enjoyed the challenge of working for a smaller-draw mountain in a state that was often an afterthought for skiing destinations.

The promised wide-open spaces to help distribute the skiers and boarders was the best benefit of all. Zooming this way and that, unencumbered by packs of people, I let the rhythmic shuddering under my skis drain the tension from my rigid limbs. Most of the time I enjoyed being boxed up in my office, pouring over spreadsheets and reports, organizing, and reconciling, but today's discovery of a miscategorized loan was a shocking worry. Gus brushed off my concern, tabling the discussion for later. The meeting left me feeling tense and in need of an escape.

When I first arrived, the financials were a mess. It had taken a month to wade through everything and figure out they were fortunate to still be open and with a full staff. That discovery led to working nonstop and making multiple adjustments. No one, not even Gus, liked the adjustments, but if he wanted to keep his company open, he had to accept them. The days of letting this resort be the "chill, cheap hang" were over. When broke college students could easily afford to ski here, something needed to change if we wanted to adhere to resort-quality ratings. Those college students spent more on pizza and beer in town than they did on lift tickets. Add to that deficit, they weren't blowing the amount they saved on lift tickets anywhere else on the resort or village grounds. It was unacceptable but not surprising, given the CEO and the COO had taken over the mountain more than thirty years ago because, "Dude, we love getting out on our sticks and boards with our buds." Resorts could no longer stay open with that attitude. Forcing them to understand that had been my biggest challenge.

With a quick kick of my heels and shift of my hips, I came to a shuddering stop near the base lodge. Snow sprayed up, the sound as comforting as the feel. It had always been this way, freeing and pacifying all at once. My early life was spent on the slopes, practicing and competing, traveling and preparing. Simple enjoyment of flinging myself down a snowy slope often escaped me. It took years away from the sport to experience that enjoyment again.

Setting my goggles up onto my ski cap, I checked out the waning crowd as the last cycle of the closest chairlift came around with the empties. It would be another twenty minutes before everyone made it down from their last runs. Two hours of work still waited for me back at my office, but I'd soak up every minute of this break.

"Doing good, Gideon," a voice called out from the gathering to my left.

Three people wobbled slightly on their skis as they watched someone inch along. One of the three lost her balance and tipped, causing the man next to her to wobble even more as she stopped her fall against him. They laughed as they righted themselves.

The bright orange mittens struck a familiar chord. The wearer spoke more encouragement again, and the familiarity kicked in. My legs stepped into a skate toward them without conscious thought.

"Hello, Blythe, good to see you again."

Her face whipped around, which caused her to tilt. My hand reached out and grasped her arm, holding her in place. "Thanks," she said automatically. "I know you. Hi, Renske." She waved to her group. "These are my roommates, Jolie and Gideon, and this is my boyfriend, Sonny." Her face flushed red, and I had the strange urge to wrap my arm around her to push away her embarrassment.

"Nice to meet you all. Getting some practice in?"

"Gideon's never skied before, and Jolie doesn't go very often."

"Well, it's a good idea to work everything out on the flats first."

"Tru said it would be okay." She leaned close and whispered, "We didn't buy tickets today."

"If you're not going on the lift, you don't need tickets." As the CFO, I shouldn't be delighted the mountain wasn't making money on these four, but something about Blythe's guileless manner made me forget my usual tenet. The bright smile she gave helped.

"Tru was going to join us, but she has a meeting."

"She knows more than we do," Sonny spoke up beside her. Dark hair with brown eyes behind old school glasses, he was attractive enough, but fell short of Blythe's league, in my opinion. Of course, her shared family resemblance with the lovely Tru probably influenced my opinion.

"Do you want some pointers?" I heard myself ask and blinked in surprise. I'd never taught anyone to ski. Certainly shouldn't be starting with an absolute beginner.

"No," Gideon said as his left ski slipped out, and he struggled to maintain his balance.

"Gideon," Jolie advised, her tone instructive, not chastising.

"Oh," he seemed to check himself, acknowledging Jolie's tone. His eyes darted over and away several times. "Maybe. Yes."

"Have you roller-skated before?" I waited for his head bob before continuing. "It's the same motion to get going. Slide out, lift, set, slide out with the other leg, lift, set, and again." I turned to Sonny. "It's easier if someone walks beside him to help keep him steady."

Sonny looked down at the bindings holding his boots. Confusion stunned him for a moment, but then he smiled and lifted his pole to push down on the release latch of a binding. In seconds he was free of his skis and clomping over to stand within reach of Gideon, who was taking slightly longer slides with his skis.

"What about you, Jolie?" I asked the girl in the puffy snowsuit. "Anything you have trouble with?"

"Stopping." She and Blythe giggled together, making everything else seem trivial.

"Don't get those two started; they'll never stop giggling," Tru called out as she climbed up the small incline to meet us.

My pulse jumped at her sudden appearance. Her hair, a study in different styles, was pleated into a thick braid today. Snowflakes clung and shimmered against the straw lowlights of her lush brown locks. She'd changed out of the skirt and sling-backs she'd worn to the office and into jeans and slip-on snow boots for her expedition outside.

"Tru!" Blythe greeted happily, her arms going out as if hugging hello was expected.

"Hi, Tru. Hey, Tru. Tru," came from the other three as she stepped into her sister's arms for a brief squeeze. Apparently, hugging hello was expected. She even hugged Jolie and wrapped an arm around Sonny's shoulders.

"Did you trap someone in your wicked web?" Tru asked her sister and Jolie, shooting amused eyes at me.

"She's helping," Blythe said, giggling again. "Aren't you going to ski with us?"

"I'll jump on the back of yours if you get going." She looked over to me with her hickory colored eyes, friendliness so apparent. It was the first thing I'd noticed about her. How open and friendly she seemed. Her demeanor served her well with her position in HR, but it wasn't just a professional mask. She was genuinely kind. All the time, which was a foreign concept to me. Being pleasant to some people took a lot of effort, and she made it seem easy. "Is this where you spend your lunch break?"

"Plan to." My lips stretched wide as they often did whenever she came by. Another foreign concept for me. Not that I didn't smile often, just not invariably and prompted by one person. I enjoyed my loner lifestyle. People tended to bother me. Yet, I looked forward to seeing Tru, no matter the type of day I was having. "Couldn't get away till last run today."

"Yay for us." Blythe pumped her fist once. "Look how good Gideon is doing."

He really hadn't made much headway, but he was taking surer strides. I wouldn't recommend adding gravity anytime soon, but he was holding steady for now.

"You're a natural, Gideon," Tru encouraged.

"How can we make Jolie stop?" Blythe looked to me instead of her sister.

I checked with Tru before answering. She'd changed clothes and come out here to help her sister and her friends, and now they were asking me for advice. Instead of the expected annoyance at being usurped, Tru looked on with open friendliness.

"Have you tried the snowplow?" I asked Jolie. She frowned and looked at Blythe. "Herringbone?" I used another term for it.

"The pizza wedge," Tru supplied, and the girls looked relieved and nodded.

"Yeah, but sometimes I get turned around and end up going backwards." She clunked her skis around and showed us her back to demonstrate.

"Reverse pizza wedge," I instructed, using the term they were familiar with. "Point the backs of your skis together and tilt your ankles in." I watched her angle the backs of her skis into a V, but then she swayed slightly.

"Or just fall down," Tru suggested as she reached forward to keep the young woman from falling. "That always stops me."

"You never fall," Sonny said.

"When I used to fall," she joked.

"And if you're going to fall, don't fight it," I shared the best tip a coach had given me. "Just sit back on your skis." Or bones break, but I didn't need to scare them.

"Good tip." Tru shot another smile at me, this one complete with those amazing dimples. It took me three months to notice those dimples and now, they're all I could see when she smiled.

"I should get back to work." I snatched my gaze away from her smile. She was a beautiful woman. I'd worked with many beautiful women. No need to get all caught up in it. And Sonny wasn't the only one punching above his weight with a Daring sister.

"Oh," Blythe said, disappointment in her tone. Then she grinned and waved, dismissing her disappointment in an instant. "Okay. Thanks, Renske."

It thrilled me how they pronounced my name correctly. Throughout school, I had to let everyone shorten my name to Ren to keep from having to constantly correct them. Most of the men I met called me Vander or Valk to avoid screwing up my first name. It was an odd name, for

Americans, anyway. My mother hadn't considered that when she'd chosen a name from her homeland of Holland.

"Happy to see you again, and to meet you all." I stepped into a slide to get moving and skated down to the staging area to take off my skis. I unbuckled my boots and clicked the ski stoppers together. Swinging them up and onto my shoulder, I started for my car to store them while I returned to work. The clunky rhythm of my booted steps usually helped me focus on the tasks at hand. This afternoon, my focus centered on how much lighter I felt from the fun encounter. I would definitely have to make this a habit. The skiing part, too.

BLESSED QUIET. My floor had emptied out an hour ago, using the "blizzard" as an excuse to leave work early. For people who loved snow, worked with snow, needed snow to keep their jobs, they sure did like to use it as an excuse for many, many things. It did, however, afford quiet time at work without interruptions.

My eyes jumped up as wind blasted against the windowpane in my office. A screen of white blocked my normal view. So, a legitimate blizzard, not hysteria, then. Well, maybe slight hysteria because it had only piled up three inches when everyone in the office started squawking about wanting to leave early. They had to close the mountain early because of the high winds, but it didn't seem necessary to empty out the office.

I stood and crossed to the window, glancing down because out was a wall of white. Close to a foot of new powder now. If the winds died down by tomorrow, it would be the best day of skiing yet. Floating red lights caught my attention as they bunched up in a line at the exit to the employee parking lot. Seems I hadn't been the only one taking advantage of the quiet in the office to get more done.

Shrugging into my coat, I sat to swap out my dress shoes for snow boots. It might be hysteria driving people to think there was too much snow to possibly work, but I wasn't stupid enough to trudge out to my car in dress shoes. Grabbing my laptop bag and gloves, I headed for the staircase. My gait halted beside the desk closest to the landing. Green and red and glitter and bows and cotton and tinsel threw up all over the desk. This hadn't been here this morning. Nor after lunch. That meant Barry or Eunice, whichever one sat at this desk, took an hour of the workday to "decorate" his or her workspace. Beyond Christmassy. This bordered on cultish devotion. Every Christmas trinket could be found on this desk. Every. Single. One. Thanksgiving was still a week off. We'd have to look at this crap for five weeks? No space was left on the desk to get work done. What was this person thinking? I couldn't help wondering if this overkill was in defiance of the mandatory holiday work schedule. They didn't like having to work, so we'd all have to suffer in a sea of tackiness.

I shook my head. Let Barry or Eunice figure out how to carve out space to work tomorrow. It wasn't my problem. He or she would be sorely disappointed with my nonreaction tomorrow morning if that had been the goal of this display. Rumor was I hated the holidays. Rumor was wrong. I had no feelings for the holidays.

Back in motion, I started my decent as a phone sounded from the floor below. At the staircase turn, it stopped and started again seconds later. Someone's cellphone, not an office phone. Was someone still here? It stopped after the fourth ring, and two steps later, started again. Someone was persistent.

The second floor was as empty as mine. Secretly I'd hoped to get a glimpse of Tru, my new favorite guilty pleasure. Something about that woman, her unrelenting pleasantness or her cheery disposition or those dimples—dimples! Naturally, she'd have alluring dimples. Whatever the reason, she was my current fascination. I'd move on, eventually, once I figured her out. At first, I thought it was mere politeness, then I attributed it to her easy nature and longstanding position in the company. Something had to explain how she could always be so, so...chipper. No, that word had an annoying connotation. Upbeat, cheery, yes, those will do. She was the kind of person who'd look at someone flipping her off and say, "Hey, he's telling me I'm #1." Not to imply she's clueless. No, just the opposite. She preferred to think the best of people. The sheer audacity of that outlook fascinated someone like me, who'd thrive in solitary confinement where most everyone else would go insane.

The ringing phone broke into my musings. I couldn't help myself, following the sound all the way to Tru's desk. Damn, she'd left her phone here, and it was ringing. Maybe she was trying to locate it, hoping she'd dropped it in her car or house somewhere.

When her desk phone rang, I jerked back, surprised after hearing the other ringtone constantly for a few minutes. It was her direct line, but still, a company phone, so I picked it up.

"Tru?" a small voice quavered on the other end.

"She's left for the day. May I take a message?"

"Oh." Wind whistled through the receiver. "I don't...I need...the buses..."

It wasn't a difficult guess. "Is this Blythe? It's Renske. What's wrong?"

"Oh, I don't know...the buses...it's cold, and Tru's not there." Her voice shook harder with each word.

"What's wrong with the buses?"

"They stopped running."

"You need to go somewhere?"

"Home," she let out a soft sob.

She wasn't home? Where was she, and why wasn't she inside instead of standing somewhere with wind blowing into her receiver? "Where are you?"

"At work."

Relief crashed through me. Strange feeling considering I'd only met her twice before. "Can you wait inside while we try to track down your sister. Does she have a home number?"

"No, just her phone, but she's not answering that."

"She left it at work, I'm afraid."

"Oh, no." A soft wail this time, and I could feel her urgency through the line.

"I'll come get you." It was the only thing that made my stomach stop twisting. "Tell me where you work." Through wind whistles and troubled hiccups, she let me know where she worked. "Don't worry. Go back inside, and I'll be there shortly."

"I can't."

"Can't what?" I was already reaching for Tru's phone to slip into my bag, knowing she'd want it.

"My boss locked the door when he left."

"You're stuck outside?" I practically shouted, heart lurching into a rapid beat. "Is there a coffee shop or café nearby? Anything you can wait inside?"

"Everything's closed. I'm at the bus stop outside my building."

"Okay, okay." I tried to keep the anger bubbling up inside from coming to the surface. What kind of place would lock their employees outside in a blizzard? A blizzard! "Can you step into the doorway of your building to get out of the wind? I'll get there as soon as I can. If anything comes up, call your sister's cell. I'm bringing it with me."

"Okay," she agreed in a quiet voice. This wasn't the happy, sweet young woman I'd met twice before. This was a freezing cold, scared girl who needed her big sister.

After signing off, I sprinted for the stairs. No dawdling to enjoy the quiet any longer. Who lets his employees, his young female employees, just stand out alone at the bus stop when bad weather is blowing through? Even I wasn't that much of a bitch boss.

I clicked the remote start on my car and exited the building. My eyes scanned the empty parking lot to make sure no one was stuck out here as I dashed to my SUV. Not bothering to use the ice scraper in the car, I plunged my hand and arm through the foot of snow built up on my windscreen and brushed it off in a snow angel sweep. Burning cold slashed at my hand and wrist, but I barely felt it. The vinyl plastered to my windscreen kept ice from forming while the car was parked outside, a trick I'd learned years ago. I reached into the car to roll down the front windows and pulled the covering off. Inside the car, the temp had risen from igloo interior to meat locker bliss with the remote start. Only the seat warmer kept me from shivering.

Snow tires and all-wheel drive punched through the berm of snow surrounding my car. Our cat operator also plowed the parking lots and the road up to the resort on snowy days. The town was responsible for the road, but we could control the schedule if we ran the plow in the morning and in the afternoon whenever necessary. I'd never been more grateful for a policy as I was today. It allowed me to race down the road as fast as safely possible.

Very few cars were still out in town, which made it easier to navigate through the driving snow and standing powder to Blythe's building. It couldn't have been more than fifteen minutes since we'd hung up, a drive that should have taken more than twenty.

A figure huddled in the shallow shelter of an office building. She was wearing a good parka, a hat, gloves, and boots, but it wouldn't matter if she'd been outside for much longer than the time it took me to get here. I skidded to a stop and jumped out of the car, urgent to get her warmed up.

"Blythe," I called to the figure.

She startled and swung around, having turned away from the bitter wind and falling snow. "Hi," she managed with a trembling voice.

"Let's get you out of here." I reached out but stopped myself from grabbing her arm. She looked frozen stiff and yanking on her might cause pain.

She took a step and stumbled on feet gone numb. My hand cupped her elbow to keep her steady. She turned and smiled with quivering lips. Every remaining chill inside me melted away with her grateful smile.

I had to open the car door when her mittened hands couldn't manage to grip the handle. The heat of the interior blasted out, and she moaned as it hit her face. With my steadying hand, she climbed up into the passenger seat. I shut the door and raced around to my side, joining her in the heated interior.

"Thank you," she said through chattering teeth.

So many things raced through my mind. Cursing her boss, cursing the buses, cursing the town, just plain cursing, but I nodded my head and said, "You're welcome."

She pushed her hands up against the vents, trying to get them warm. Her glasses fogged up and snowflakes melted and dripped from her knit hat.

I reached out and pulled off her matching mittens. "Stick your hands under your rump."

Even though she was clearly distressed, rubbed raw by the cold and the despair of being stranded, she giggled. Giggled! She may be even more fascinating than her beautiful sister. "Ooo, seat warmers." Her voice still quavered, but her body relaxed against the seat.

"May I?" I reached for her glasses and held up the cleaning cloth from my sunglasses case. She nodded, and I spent the next few moments carefully wiping her glasses clean before placing them back on her face. "Better?"

"Mm-hmm," she sighed, head resting against the seat, eyes closed. "Wish Tru's car had seat warmers."

How was it possible Tru lived in a ski town without seat warmers in her car? Winter weather package add-ons shouldn't be out of anyone's salary range in this town. A review of staff salaries would now top my to-do list for next week.

I shook my head of the unimportant reminder for now. "Ready to go home?"

Her head shook, but it took a minute before she said, "I wanna go see Tru."

I'd been hoping she'd say that. "Sure thing."

She gave me directions through town and into one of the older neighborhoods where a mix of styles made for the ultimate ski town quaintness. We pulled into the driveway of a small Tudor. I'd barely shut off the engine before Blythe had the door pushed open, and she was scrambling toward the front door.

Tru came out onto the front stoop in time to catch her sister in a welcome hug. When it turned into a shuddering mass of sobs, I moved from my stance next to the car to help explain. Tru's eyes widened when she caught sight of me. I couldn't blame her. I'd be freaked if she just showed up on my doorstep as well.

"You forgot your phone at work, and Blythe needed a ride. She's still warming up. Should we go inside?"

"Oh, honey," she crooned, shuffling them backwards into the house. "Did the buses go to the snow routes? I'm so sorry I forgot my phone and you couldn't reach me."

Blythe was murmuring softly as she let her sister guide her into the house. Clearly, Blythe had managed to hold it together just long enough to get to her big sister.

I followed them inside the cozy space. "Bathroom? I'll start a bath, best way to get warm."

Tru looked up from helping her sister pull off her boots. "Good idea. Up the stairs, last door on the left. Thanks." She turned back to Blythe. "How about that, Blythe? A nice bath will warm you up."

"I know." Her head nodded in agreement.

I dashed up the stairs to get a bath started. I was being entirely presumptuous, but it felt good to take care of someone. Someone completely open and trusting, without the dread of wondering what they'd feel they had to do to pay it back.

The bathroom was tight but big enough for a clawfoot tub. So much better than the modern square thing in the master bath at my townhouse. I twisted the faucets and got the water flowing, reaching down to plug the stopper. Bath salts lined the shelf, but I'd let Blythe choose which ones to add if she wanted.

Downstairs the sisters were still wrapped together. Tru was rubbing her hands up and down Blythe's arms, repeating, "Everything's okay now," over and over. Their close relationship was a thing of envy. As an only child, I'd never known anything like it.

Tru's eyes landed on mine as I hit the bottom step. "Bath is filling up."

"Thank you, and thank you for bringing Blythe home."

"I happened to be leaving the office at the exact right time to hear the phone."

"Lucky us, right, Blythe?" Tru encouraged her sister to respond.

"She answered your phone at work and came to get me. She was really fast. And she has seat warmers."

Tru smiled in relief. This sounded a lot more like the Blythe I'd met. "Ready for that bath?" She got Blythe standing and headed toward the staircase. I started for the door, but one glance from Tru told me to sit my ass down and stay.

It took a few minutes for her to return. "I can't believe this happened. She's usually able to leave before the buses go to snow routes."

"It's not just that; she wasn't able to get back into her building."

She blew a fierce breath through her nose. "It's an offsite location for them. There's a part-time custodian, a security guard, and her boss there. Her boss is a dickless wonder who exerts the only power he'll ever have in life over her and the custodian."

I bit back a laugh. "That's the first time I've heard you be negative about anything."

"Right," she chuckled, and those dimples flashed again.

My eyes zeroed in automatically. For a moment, an embarrassing moment, I clenched my fist and pressed it against my thigh to keep from reaching out to trace the fetching divots. "I'd better get going if I'm going to make it home before the roads get really bad."

Her eyes darted to the window and widened. "Of course. I can't thank you enough."

"It was a ride." I brushed off the gratitude as she walked me to the door.

Her hand reached out and gripped mine. Warm, soft, perfectly fitted. Knowing that made it more difficult to leave. "It was more than that. Thank you."

"See you tomorrow." I released her hand and stepped outside, away from the warmth of her dazzling smile and into the cold where I lived most of my life.

THE FAMILY reached for their hot beverages all at once, practically pushing each other out of the way for the jolt of caffeine that would allow them to continue skiing on a day when most other Americans were clustered around the dining room eating turkey and annoying each other. An hour into my floating shift at the coffee stand, I was ready to float over to something else. People were really particular about their coffee, and what was a seven-year-old doing getting an espresso? Was that even legal?

"Sucks you have to work on Thanksgiving," the older brother of the seven-year-old caffeine bandit commented as he took a large gulp of his overly complicated coffee mixture.

Yeah, but not enough for you to consider that before deciding to vacation on a holiday, thus forcing the necessity for people to work on a holiday. Wouldn't it be lovely to live in a world where I could say that to the snotty teen? The only reason they were taking a break from skiing was to satisfy his coffee demand. Not exaggerating, he demanded coffee, and his parents were proud to relay that information to me.

Kids. Not a whole lot better than people.

"You're late," I informed the barista as she rushed into the coffee peddling square.

The position of the coffee kiosk bothered me the first time I walked into the lodge. From a marketing perspective, it was genius. Most people have a difficult time walking past their twice or thrice daily habit, even if they weren't craving coffee. In practice, though, lines formed on every side, not only congesting the area, but also angering people in the slower lines. Many ended up abandoning their place and going over to the village for their coffee fix. This was one of many suggested changes added to my list. When Gus was ready to hear them, it would be a long meeting.

"I know, I'm sorry," the barista gushed, wrapping her apron around her waist. "Time got away from me. The whole family was over, and I couldn't hear my phone alarm."

Or you continually ignored it, thinking your colleague would cover for you because you're a gap year lay-about who thinks only of herself. One good thing came from floating duties today: personnel dynamics were on display and easily analyzed. She wasn't the only one pushing the limits on Tru's carefully planned out holiday schedule. The people manning the lift ticket office and equipment rental counters all left fifteen minutes early. Only one cook showed up, and two cafeteria servers cut out for a half hour on their shifts. So far, the only people working without complaint for their full shifts were the hotel staff, who were used to working holidays, and all the mountain positions. Still, I was looking forward to my last hour of the day helping to cover a lift line.

Donning my parka, gloves, and headband ear warmer, I made my way out of the lodge and onto the staging area of the mountain. One more hour till closing, the ski crowds were winding down. The morning had been packed, but with the afternoon eating and football watching, even vacationing families were taking part in the more traditional holiday festivities. Many of the local restaurants were holding holiday feasts, and every bar in town had some kind of viewing celebration. I'd considered stopping to pick up something resembling a real dinner before going home, but after the long day, a microwaved meal was the most effort I was willing to put forth.

"So, despite changing the policy to make everyone share in the hours on the holidays, a policy that made you extremely unpopular, you still put in a full day's shift." The voice was lighthearted but also curious.

I turned to see Tru walking toward me. She had her hair pulled back into a ponytail that swished against her shoulder blades, and a headband covered her ears to keep the chill away. She wore jeans and a turtleneck under the familiar green company parka, which looked far less plain on her than it did on me. Nothing about her was plain.

"You're working the shift least populated yourself." As soon as my policy was implemented, every HQ staffer put in requests for the morning shift to get home for the afternoon.

"Yes, but thanks to you, I'm only on for three hours instead of nine or ten."

"Not everyone's putting in their full shift." I muttered, glancing back to the lodge where I'd spent my whole day.

"I'm just happy they put in an hour or two. Three was almost too much to wish for."

That outlook of hers. Silver linings everywhere. Would life be easier with that kind of outlook or just a lot more work? "What have you been doing?"

"Lift lines."

My head nodded, happy that she'd been able to enjoy the beautiful sunny day and usually happy crowds as opposed to the guests indoors, who could be cranky and demanding. "Good gig."

"It has been. I'm swapping with Mina. She's helping guests organize their departure."

"I didn't know we had that position."

"We don't normally, but we want people leaving when the mountain closes today. Staff can assist guests with getting their skis, boards, poles, and kids collected and set off in the right direction. People don't linger if employees are silently herding them toward the exit."

"And we all get to go home at a decent hour. Nice."

"Speaking of," she started and dipped her head, hiding her weather burned cheeks for a moment. "My sister and I are having dinner around six-thirty if you don't have plans. She's babysitting the turkey right now. Her boyfriend will be there, and my neighbors always pop in. You're more than welcome, and I know Blythe would love to see you again. She was disappointed you had to leave before she could thank you the other day."

I waved off the concern. "She already did, and like I said, it was just a ride."

"Well, I won't pry about your plans. You know where we live, so if you find yourself in our area tonight, stop by." She glanced away and raised a gloved hand to wave at someone behind me. Was it my imagination or had her cheeks gotten redder? "Hope you can make it. If not, enjoy the rest of your shift."

Indulging in one of my favorite pastimes, I watched her walk away until she was out of sight. Gorgeous. It was the first thing I noticed about her, then she opened her mouth and became even more lovely with the way she treated people. Her Thanksgiving plans sounded mellow. I thought she'd be hosting all the Thanksgiving orphans at her table, but no, only a few. And me. Must have been the unorthodox but highly emotional day on Monday that prompted the invitation.

Amazingly, for just a moment, I wanted to go. Really wanted to go. I'd never been to anyone's for Thanksgiving before. With a native Dutch mother, we never celebrated this holiday. It wasn't a thing, but today, imagining what one would be like for Tru and Blythe, it was tempting.

"'Bout time," the guy watching two skiers slip into place before the chairlift swung around to scoop them up griped as I darted between the moving chairs to stand next to him. He'd worked all of three hours in one of the least taxing positions for someone used to working in IT. If he'd had to spend even ten minutes waiting on people at the coffee square, he would have quit on the spot. Tru really knew where best to spread the resources we had today.

"I'm five minutes early." I could be a petty asshole, too. "Hello there," I greeted the twosome moving into position for the next chair. "Enjoy your run." I looked back at the IT schmuck. "I'll take it from here."

He stomped off after not getting whatever reaction he'd wanted from me. "Iceberg," he muttered as he walked away.

If he were one of the few HQ employees I admired, I'd be hurt by his jab. I knew how I came across to a lot of people. Stoicism wasn't a common American trait, especially not with women. It automatically made us bitches—cold bitches, frigid, unyielding, but mostly, bitches. I'd heard it all my life. These employees had a wide range of names to call me, and for the most part, it didn't bother me. I was still new and making unpopular changes. They needed an outlet, but once the company's finances evened out and the changes made work better for everyone on staff, they'd hopefully ease up.

"Having a good day?" I asked the next couple sliding into place. The man tipped as he overdid the skidding stop. My hand steadied him as the chair swung into his knees, forcing his rump to drop gracelessly onto the seat before it started up the hill.

"Happy Thanksgiving," a female twosome sang out as they slipped into place for the chair. And that's how the next hour of my day went.

The mounted radio squawked as I was still turning people away ten minutes after close. It announced the lift was clear of guests. I waved two ski patrollers and four mountain safety guides into the line and loaded them onto the lift. They'd ski through the available runs from the top of the lift, making sure to clear this part of the mountain of skiers

The radio squawked again, allowing me to shut down the lift. Grabbing a snow shovel, I scraped, moved, and packed snow to even out the loading zone. Ruts caused skiers to trip, which was dangerous with the swinging chairs.

By the time I put up the shovel, several patrollers had already made it down to the base lodge. Several guests were stepping out of skis and boards, collecting their poles and backpacks, ready to lug everything to their cars. It hadn't taken long to clear the mountain today. Probably everyone ready to get to a holiday meal.

I headed for the lodge again. The coffee counter would be slammed with to-go orders. I spotted Tru showing three kids how to carry their skis more easily. Nothing but smiles all around while she instructed and answered questions and issued parting words to guests as they sauntered off toward their cars. She'd probably stay until the last person was gone, even if she was off duty in another ten minutes.

My attention was drawn to the lines around the coffee square. As expected, three shuttle loads of people were waiting in line. The payroll clerk helping out the barista who'd been late looked ready to pull out his hair. I jumped into action, letting him take orders and play cashier while I helped the barista make the simpler drinks.

It took forty-five minutes to clear the lines and put up a closed sign. After helping to clean the coffee machines and the countertop, I trudged over to my office to get some work done. No other cars were left in the employee parking lot as I walked past, which should be a hint for me to go home. It wasn't like the work wouldn't be here tomorrow.

My thoughts drifted to the holiday season. Never my favorite, and not because I was alone. People made a big deal about the holidays, and yet after they were over, the complaining began. Arguments they had, weight they gained, lousy presents they received. No one ever seemed to enjoy them, but the buildup was frenzied. Made me shake my head every year.

Losing concentration, I sighed and shut down my computer. Might as well go home. I'd been on my feet all day, and my facial muscles were sore from smiling at guests. I could heat up some soup, make a salad, play the viola for a while, and maybe find an old movie to watch tonight. A far less stressful holiday than most people were spending.

The streets teamed with people and cars. Many restaurants and bars were open for tourists to take advantage. Locals were going to or coming home from holiday festivities. My eyes glanced down at the clock on my dash. Tru's dinner was underway. I could still make it.

Holidays. Families. No. Not for me. I wouldn't know how to act. What if she found out I was the rigid bitch most of her colleagues thought I was? Right now, she didn't mind my company. Seemed to enjoy chatting with me. Sought me out to say hello. One night set against such warm, cheerful people, of course I'd stand out. How could I not?

At the stop sign, it was a right turn to her house and a left turn to my townhouse. My hands pulled left on the steering wheel, habit and comfort deciding for me. Five minutes later, I parked in the one car garage on the ground level of my corner unit.

Heading up the stairs, I could hear laughter and music coming over from the place next door. This was one of the major downsides of living in a townhome. It never mattered how well soundproofed the shared wall, noise still leaked through. They were good neighbors, but for the bi-monthly dinner parties. As long as I turned up my stereo or television, I could drown out the noise.

The refrigerator was pretty bare. Salad and soup didn't hold much appeal, but it was that or a frozen vegetarian lasagna dinner. My eyes went to the viola standing upright in the corner of my living room. I could play for a while, that always drained my stress, but my arms ached from overuse today.

My rump slid onto a stool at the kitchen island. Fingers drummed the granite countertop. Boredom. My worst enemy. Usually I had work to occupy my thoughts. A good book, playing the viola, watching TV, skiing, snowmobiling, cross-country or any number of other outside activities did the same. But tonight, I didn't want to do any of those things. Tonight, I only thought about one thing.

"You made it," Tru's happy voice and smile greeted me when she opened the door of her home. Nothing in her tone or expression showed displeasure at my being an hour and a half late.

"Renske!" Blythe yelped and footsteps pounded down the hallway. She slid to a stop on her stocking feet, gripping her sister's waist before she slid right out through the door and into me. She probably wouldn't have minded if my hands weren't full with a bottle of wine and two bakery boxes. "Happy Thanksgiving!"

"And for you as well," I returned her greeting. My eyes went to Tru. "I wanted to stop by and thank you for the invitation."

"Come inside, we'll make up a plate."

"I'm late for dinner. I really just wanted to say hello to everyone and drop off some dessert."

Blythe tugged on my arm. "Join us. Sonny wants seconds. We can all eat again."

"I'll just say hello." My feet followed orders my subconscious was issuing.

"What kind?" Blythe reached for the pie boxes.

"Guess."

She laughed and lifted the boxes to her nose, but Tru snatched them away before she could get a hint. It made her laugh harder. Her boyfriend moved to stand next to her, joining laughter even without knowing the reason why.

"Cherry, please?"

Her hopefulness made us all laugh again. "You guessed one. You're very good at this guessing game."

"Pumpkin," Sonny tried, patting his thick stomach. My head shake did nothing to diminish his pleasure.

"Avocado," Tru threw out a bad guess intentionally so as not to ruin the fun for her sister.

"Apple?" Blythe asked.

"You are a pie psychic," I told her. "Will they do?"

"Yes!" Sonny agreed.

"Perfect," Tru added. "Thank you for bringing them."

"I hope I didn't spoil your planned dessert."

"There's never too much dessert," Blythe said and went into the kitchen for some plates.

Tru pulled a partially carved turkey from the refrigerator and several bowls. In moments, she had two full plates loaded and two other plates with much smaller portions. She placed them to heat in the oven, then held out a corkscrew to me.

Once again, my body was doing things my subconscious clearly wanted when my conscious was telling me to politely decline and let this happy little family get on with their holiday. My hand accepted the corkscrew and went to work opening the wine I'd brought.

When I poured four glasses, Tru shot me a grateful smile. Before I could ask what earned me the smile, a timer dinged, and she turned away to pull the plates from the oven. Blythe guided me to a chair, and everyone sat to a second dinner.

"The turkey's dry. I let it cook too long," Blythe reported, looking dejected.

I finished swallowing the admittedly dry piece of turkey. "This is the best turkey dinner I've ever had." It was the only turkey dinner I'd ever had, but still, the best.

"It's delicious," Sonny said like a good boyfriend should.

"You did good, sis," Tru complimented.

"Thanks." Blythe blushed and pushed her glasses up in an embarrassed gesture. "I can't wait for the pies."

"Why wait?" I asked because I was new to this holiday dinner tradition. It wasn't like she was a small child who needed to finish her dinner before she could have dessert, and they'd already had dinner, anyway.

Blythe's eyes widened and shot to her sister's. They both grinned and raced each other to the oven where the pies were warming. The sight made me laugh and all the boredom and hollowness I'd experienced when I stepped into my townhouse vanished. Maybe there was something to this holiday thing.

Or maybe it was just the company of a sweet young woman and her gorgeous sister.

OUTSIDE MY office, voices murmured and mumbled and generally kept their owners from working. We made it through the first of the major winter holidays and no one could stop talking about it. Even three days later. Mine had been particularly delightful, but I wasn't out there yapping on and on about it. Not that anyone would believe me if I did.

"At least you didn't have to be around Frozen the entire day."

"Neither did you, drama queen."

"An hour with Gelid is more than enough."

"You'd get frostbite if you had to spend more time with Nippy."

Did they think I was too stupid to realize they were talking about me, or did they not care if I could hear? Perhaps they didn't understand the concept of sound and how it traveled. They usually only did this when they were certain I wasn't in my office, but the carefree atmosphere over the past few days had loosened their tongues. And Gelid? Someone spent some time on a thesaurus site. I'd heard virtually every synonym of the words "cold" and "frigid" over the past six months from everyone here, except Tru. Tru didn't use names like that for people. Could be her optimistic nature, or could be she didn't think of me that way. I liked her optimism, but her possible positive impression of me made my insides buzz.

"She's not that bad," someone who sounded like Diego said, and the office floor went quiet. "What? She helped me shovel the walkways. A total crap job, and she shoveled more than I did. That's okay by me. Remember our last boss? That dude pawned all his work off onto us. I'm just saying."

Nice, Diego. One down, a couple dozen more of these coworkers to go.

"Valk," the intercom on my office phone announced. "You got a minute?"

Aiden's code for: get your ass in here and solve an issue between me and Gus. It was never a good idea to ignore the request. I saved my last entries and closed the laptop. Every head turned and followed my stroll across the floor to Gus's office. At some point they'd have to start giving me a break, wouldn't they?

"Cost out adding more shuttles," was the greeting Gus gave me when I stepped into his office.

"It's not worth it," Aiden argued, and I agreed, but wouldn't say so right away. We ran shuttles every half hour for tourists and locals in town to save on parking spaces and traffic on the two-lane road up to the mountain. Every ski town had them. Some shared the cost with the town; this place shouldered the whole cost. Yet another cost-cutting change on my list, and so far, Gus hadn't made any strides toward starting negotiations with the town.

"I can run a customer acquisition cost analysis for each shuttle. Are you talking about another shuttle at the open and the close or for the whole day?" It wouldn't matter, not for this expense.

"Do both," Gus ordered. "We've got to monetize more things around here."

Adding free shuttles was the exact opposite of monetizing an expense outlay. "We should consider adding a ski-through coffee cart outside. A lot of mountains have them now. It'll have to be a mobile cart or temporary shelter until a fully operational building can be constructed in the summer, but even if we just serve from two coffee urns, we'd see a nice intake each day."

"Do people buy plain coffee these days?" Aiden asked, genuine curiosity on his face.

"People do." Half my time at the coffee square on Thursday was spent drawing those drinks. "And they don't want to get out of their skis and tromp into the lodge to get them. Offer medium cups and thermos refills and several hours of every shift should be pure profit. I'll run the numbers to find the break-even."

"I like it," Gus declared. That was one thing about these guys. They didn't beat around the bush with compliments or criticism.

"I'll get right on that." I left them to their continued discussions about snow conditions, football, poker night, or any of their other usuals. According to office gossip, they'd lost interest in the day-to-day running of the resort a few years ago. As long as things ran smoothly, they let everyone be. When something breaks down or complaints come in, they often make rash decisions to fix the problem as quickly as possible. That kind of problem-solving caused many financial setbacks, which necessitated the search for a new CFO. I should be grateful for their hasty and short-sighted maneuvers because it led to my hiring, but my job often felt like trying to keep a teenager from using the "emergency" credit card for a concert and an after-party kegger.

The chatter hadn't died down by my return. Halfway back, I spotted a cluster around one of the desks. Laughter erupted before everyone broke apart, leaving the webmaster at his desk with Tru leaning against it. She'd been the one to encourage everyone back to work, somehow managing the task without being a bossy B about it. She was their colleague, but they all listened to her and respected her. So far, I hadn't seen the same with her boss.

"Hi, Renske," she greeted, completely unaware of the social faux pas she just committed, or completely uncaring. Everyone would forgive her this kindness; they'd chalk it up to her unrelenting sunny nature.

"Hello, Tru." I tried to keep my tone entirely professional, but it was difficult. It wasn't just that I'd been in her home twice, been cared for by both her and her sister. She drew me in, and I wasn't fighting it anymore.

"Could I have a minute?" she asked.

She could have years, if she wanted them. I gestured toward my office, leaving the door open so as not to add to the list of topics my colleagues could discuss to avoid more work.

"Went by my sister's workplace yesterday to pick her up." Her eyes bored into mine, expectation making the hickory color shine brightly. "Saw her boss." Again, the expectant look. "Had an interesting chat with him."

I couldn't look away, even as heat burned my cheeks. I had an interesting chat with him as well. One that wasn't my place to have, but I didn't care. Blythe was more than just kind to me. She was a sweet woman, who was being taken advantage of, and I wouldn't stand for it.

"He practically groveled at my feet. Admitted he screwed up leaving Blythe at the bus stop like that. It would never happen again. He'd already apologized to Blythe. It was a lot of groveling without any provocation on my part."

"Like you said, he's a small-minded dick who wants to wield what little power he has, and now he's seen the error of his ways."

"With help from you." She didn't accuse me of anything. She was stating a fact, and she didn't seem upset that I'd stuck my nose into her sister's business.

"Blythe forgot her mittens in my car. He happened to be there when I dropped them off, and we might have had some words."

She chuckled and dropped into the seat facing my desk. A head toss swept her chestnut tresses back over her shoulders. "I'll say. He said you threatened to sue him for negligence."

Little dickweed tattletale. "I told him about my attorney friend who takes on negligence cases. I never actually said I'd sue him." If he inferred that, well, his problem, not mine. Our conversation went over how he'd known full well the buses had gone to snow routes when he watched Blythe trot down the sidewalk to the nearby bus stop, which was a mile off the snow route. He knew she'd wait and wait and wait until she figured out the buses weren't just late, but not coming. For him to lock the building and drive off in his car, leaving a young woman alone in the dark snowstorm was beyond misconduct for a supervisor. If Blythe would let me, I'd insist his boss fire him. But Blythe wasn't like that. She thought this was the best job she'd ever had. After describing her other two jobs, one as a busser for a fast food restaurant, and the other, cleaning the bathrooms at the community center, yeah, being a file clerk at a medical practice storage facility was better.

"Well, he's calmed down and started treating her like he treats the other two employees there, which is to say, as if they barely exist."

Not exactly ideal, but better than how he treated her before. It was a pleasure knocking his superior attitude down a peg. "If she had another job opportunity, would she consider leaving?"

Tru tensed, worry bunching her shoulders. "She likes her routines. She knows this job, even if it's far less interesting than when she first started with a different boss. She can get there and back on her own. It pays a dollar more than minimum wage. And the last time she looked for another job, you should have seen how the hiring managers would react when they'd come out to the waiting area and call her name for the interview. I don't understand why some people can't see her for who she is, not her syndrome."

A lump formed in my throat. The idea that anyone would automatically write off Blythe angered me, and I wasn't her protective, older sister. "That attorney friend of mine has been looking for a competent file clerk for three years. They've tried hiring several people, but no one can stick to it. The work is meticulous, something most people don't have patience for. They confuse meticulous with monotonous. Something tells me Blythe wouldn't."

"It sounds amazing." She paused to consider the offer. "Blythe loves organizing, but it's hard to get her to try something new."

"If it's okay, I'll bring it up the next time I see her."

A slow grin crept across her face, dimples starting as specks and then digging deeper into her cheeks. "You are a wonderful person, Renske Van der Valk."

I pushed out an amused breath, waving off the compliment. "You're putting way too much weight on a job connection."

Her hand reached across the desk, landing on top of mine. Warm tingles spread from the point of contact. My hand clenched into a fist under hers. Tightness overtook the tingles, which seemed like a metaphor for my life.

BLYTHE'S EYES nervously flicked to me as I pulled into the parking lot of my friend's law office. She finally agreed to consider a new job only after Tru and I promised to try it out with her. Tru thought she'd be more confident about quitting her current job if she knew she could do this new one. My friend was all too happy to let us come in on a Saturday if it led to someone filling the open job slot.

"What if I can't do the job?" Blythe's nerves finally surfaced verbally.

"Of course, you can," Tru encouraged.

As wonderful as Tru's support was, I didn't think blind encouragement was what Blythe needed to hear. "Not everyone is perfect for every job. Just ask your sister who has to find the right people for the right jobs all the time. Sometimes, she can tell when she interviews them, and sometimes, it takes a while on the job before everyone figures it out." My hand flicked to the two-story triangular building filling the corner lot in front of us. "That's why we're here today. We'll give this a try to see if you like it. You may not, but you will like my friend." I opened the car door to prompt them to do the same. If someone told me spending a Saturday afternoon in a file room would be topping my list of desired weekend activities, I'd think someone needed to stop talking.

"Ren," Penny greeted us at the door. We met several years ago as neighbors. She moved here after her fiancé got a job offer and threw out a shingle for her law practice. Within four years, she'd taken on three partners. We'd kept in touch, mostly through email until she told me about the open CFO position here. Now, I got to see her in person whenever I liked.

"Hi, Penny, let me introduce you to my friends, Blythe and Tru."

"Welcome. Nice to meet you both." She led us through reception and into the office area. An open desk layout filled the space. Several conference rooms lined the walls, bordered by offices for the senior associates. "I was thrilled when Ren said she might know someone for this position. We haven't had much luck."

"I don't know if I can do it," Blythe admitted, her nerves flaring again. Tru slid her hand into her sister's and gave her an encouraging squeeze.

"All I ask is that you give it a try and see." Penny said the exact right thing, not that I'd been worried. She had a knack for it, one of the skills that made her an excellent attorney. She took us through the space, waving at two attorneys in occupied offices. "They're working on trial prep right now. When they have a break, I'll introduce you."

Tru and Blythe looked at each other, surprise showing on their faces. They probably thought Blythe might be relegated to the basement or another building and have no interaction with anyone else like in her current job. The layout here wasn't like that, nor were the people. Just one more tick on the positive side of the pros and cons list for this job.

We stepped into the file room, a large space with rows of shelves taking up the back two-thirds of the room. In front of us were two L-shaped desks set against the windows on opposite sides of the room. Each desk had its own monitor, printer, and scanner.

Penny gestured to the desks. "One of these will be yours. You'll be opening files for our new cases, organizing files to get them trial ready, and closing them down for storage. We've started digitizing our backlog of files, and we'll be offering that service to other organizations. You'd scan every page of every file, check to make sure all the scanned documents are readable, then shred the paper copy."

Blythe's eyes grew wider and wider and darted to her sister repeatedly. I stepped in before her increasing panic made her want to leave without trying the job. "Whoa, Penny, you're moving way too fast for me."

She laughed and patted my shoulder. "Sorry, I got excited there for a minute. That's just an overview to give you an idea of what's in store. Some days it'll only be organizing and filing. Other days it'll be scanning. It's not all at once."

"That sounds okay, doesn't it, Blythe?" Tru looped an arm around her sister.

"Yeah." Blythe still sounded nervous.

"New jobs are always intimidating," I told her. "The only thing that made sense on my first day at the mountain was your sister's orientation meeting."

Tru smiled, knowing I was exaggerating but not about to call me on it. "Let's try a little bit of everything."

"Great." Penny rubbed her hands together and darted forward to grab a legal box off one of the shelves. She placed it on one of the desks, then turned and grabbed several file folders, labels, and separators. "Okay, this will be the majority of what you'd do, day in and day out." She started going through instructions again, and I could tell it would get overwhelming quickly. Tru had explained to me how Blythe could shutdown whenever things came at her too fast. It was one of the main reasons she stuck to her job with the asshat boss.

"You know what I like to do when I get a new task?" I asked, surprising Penny with the interruption. She was the talker in our friendship. I added comments and opinions when she came up for air. It worked for us. Interruptions were rare.

"What?" Blythe responded, desperate for a break in the barrage of info coming her way.

"I write down every step so I have something handy to double check along the way. What do you think? I'll be the scribbler, and you both follow along with Penny?"

The look Tru gave me caused a pulse of arousal in the pit of my stomach. She wanted to touch me in some way to express her gratitude. I could give her multiple suggestions on ways to touch me, but now was not the time. Penny could only give us a couple of hours today. We needed to make the most of it to get Blythe to the point where she'd feel comfortable switching to this job. My suddenly laser focused libido could wait.

I brought out my phone to record Penny's rapid-fire speech pattern. She started with step-by-step procedures on opening a new case file, showing how the files were labeled, sectioned, and organized. Tru and Blythe had fun following each direction, punching holes in client info sheets, inserting separators in each folder, and adding the case number to the database on the computer. They moved onto the scanning procedures, which was a little more involved and required attention to detail. I could easily see why her previous hires would screw this up. Very few people would painstakingly check each document was scanned properly. Blythe wouldn't be careless when it came to that.

"It's too fast. I'll mess up." Blythe said softly, clearly upset.

"That's the beauty of this position, Blythe," Penny jumped in before Tru could ease her mind. "Scanning can be done at your own pace. All of these files are closed cases. We want them digitized to be able to reference easily. Until then, we've still got the paper copy to look up what we need. So, there's no rush on the scanning project. Okay?"

Blythe nodded, looking more relieved. "No rush."

"Hey, Pen," an attorney came into the file room, halting when she saw the room was filled with people. "Oh, hey, Ren, what's up?"

I gestured to Blythe. "We're showing Blythe, here, what a typical day would be like for a file clerk."

"Oh, yes, please!" Virginia sighed dramatically. Dramatically was pretty much her default setting. "Please say you'll come to our rescue here, Blythe. We've needed a file clerk for ages."

Penny chuckled at her law partner. "Virginia is one of the few attorneys constantly looking for trial nuggets in our closed case files. She's also one of the few attorneys who can't alphabetize."

Virginia snorted and smacked Penny's shoulder. "She's right. Before every trial, my paralegal is resorting my files because documents are always out of order." She moved past us to the shelves, grabbing a file box and bringing it over to the other desk. Popping the lid, she flipped through the files inside and grabbed one. "Anyway, we sure could use your help. I hope you take the job, Blythe." She waved the file folder in her hand and disappeared back out into the office area.

Penny looked over at the open box and pointed. "And that's also part of the job. You'll get paralegals and legal secretaries in here rooting through the files and using this other desk, but they'll always return the files. Some of the partners, though, are so focused on their current case, they forget to return boxes to their proper location. You'll have to put them back, otherwise this desk will be overrun with case files."

For the next two hours, we went through all the possible tasks several times so Blythe would be comfortable with them. I'd still type up all the instructions for her to reference, which should give her that extra boost of confidence if she takes the job.

As we loaded back into my car, I asked, "Do you have an initial impression?"

"Everyone's nice," Blythe said.

"I liked the workspace." Tru edged forward from the backseat and patted her sister's shoulder.

"I like the location," I added, pointing out the bus stop a few feet away. It was on the snow route for buses, and the street was lined with other businesses and places to go for lunch or drinks after work.

"I like Penny," Tru added.

"I like all her partners," I joined in. This must be how Tru eased Blythe into making new things less scary.

"I like..." Blythe began and thought for a moment, "that all the papers need to be in order."

"Blythe likes organizing," Tru announced proudly.

"I like the desk. It would be mine alone. No sharing."

"I like that you don't have to clock in and out," Tru said, which was surprising because more than half our staff had to use a timecard app to keep track of their hours. But I could see where the salaried position at this job would be easier and more secure.

"I like the job," Blythe said after taking everything in.

"Good. Sleep on it for a few nights and see if you feel the same way," I encouraged. "You heard Penny, the job is yours if you want it."

"Thank you, Renske. I had fun with you today."

I glanced over at my young charge and smiled. We'd done two hours of honest work at my friend's office and she characterized it as fun. My eyes searched out Tru's in the rearview mirror. She returned my gaze, something secretive hidden there. I liked those secrets and what they seemed to promise.

"NO CHRISTMAS party?" Gus showed me eyes the size of manhole covers as if I'd forbidden him from skiing for the rest of his life. "You can't be serious."

I assumed it was a rhetorical question. It sounded like a rhetorical question and also like something professional tennis players shouted at line judges. Since it was directed at me—someone perpetually serious, or so they thought—it had to be rhetorical.

"What's your hang-up with Christmas?" Aiden glanced up at me from his tipped back position in the chair next to mine.

"Don't have one." I didn't bother looking at him. This was supposed to be a meeting dedicated to cost-cutting, and they'd fixated on one line-item from the start. Obsessed over it.

"We've got to have a party. It's expected."

"That may be, but it's not in the budget." Not just a missing line-item, it genuinely could not be added to the budget without pushing us into the red.

"We've never had a budget."

My eyes bounced from Gus to Aiden and back to Gus. They didn't seem to get how not having a budget was exactly what landed them in a position last year where they'd had to postpone payroll for three weeks until more revenues came in. The finance department used to consist of one full-time bookkeeper, who preferred paper ledgers, and two part-time bookkeepers, who attempted to transfer everything to digital records with a poorly designed and flawed spreadsheet. Their boss had been a yes-man for Gus and Aiden, agreeing to all their wild money-generating ideas and expensive solutions to any issues that arose. He must have had some financial savvy because he bailed before it got really bad. Had I known the state of the finances at my interview, I would have looked much more carefully at the other CFO posting in the Sierras.

"At the start we did, but after, we didn't need one," Aiden reminded him.

Probably not. They would have been able to pull in big bucks with a skeletal crew on a mountain known for day skiing rather than a resort destination. A hotelier added the inn, leasing the property until the resort bought it out six years ago. A commercial developer put in the village, annually leasing the property. For years, they were making buckets of cash with little outlay until competition from other full-service resorts forced them to offer amenities and services without doing a cost-benefit analysis. It was at that point, they started adding layers of management to bring in more skills and innovation to expand. Payroll became the unwieldy beast on the P&L statement. Their former CFO shuffled expenses around as much as he could but finally ditched the job when he saw the black hole at the end of the tunnel.

"You need and have one now. Over the next year, I'll be asking each department to make up their own budgets to further account for every dollar spent. For this year, I've pieced together your actual budget expenditures and made a forecast to get us to the profit margins we need. Actual and forecast are a long way apart. Your holiday parties are not part of the forecast budget as it stands. If we come up with more revenue streams, we can add back the parties." Simple math. If you have the money, you can spend the money. If you don't, well, you get the picture.

"Grinch, huh?" Aiden joked. Like his best friend, he'd started growing what would become an unruly hipster beard. Both were far too old to consider themselves hipsters, but this seemed to be the trend in ski towns these days.

I shot a bored look at him. Just because I hadn't participated in the Memorial Day BBQ or the Fourth's fireworks or the Labor Day picnic or the Halloween haunted house didn't mean I hated the holidays. We couldn't afford to host those events either, and when my advice was ignored, I didn't feel right about helping the company waste more money by attending.

"As I've recommended before, the budget doesn't have room for any of your parties. You throw employee parties practically every month, but none is more extravagant than your Christmas party."

"You can't just take away our biggest party a couple weeks before it happens," Gus complained. At fifty-nine, he did a damn good impression of a petulant teen when he wanted.

"I'm not taking anything away. I'm telling you, we can't afford it. If you want to put it on your personal credit cards, go for it."

"Not gonna happen," Aiden snarked. Rumor said he spent most of his salary on child support for his four kids, alimony for his two ex-wives, and maintenance for his twenty-six-year-old girlfriend.

Gus glared at him. They'd been best friends since college, and Aiden's wives, mistresses, and now girlfriend have all made memorable appearances on the resort grounds over the years. Gus has been married for nearly thirty years and had three kids, seemingly the exact opposite of his best friend. "How much would it be?"

He didn't even know how much they spent on their Christmas parties? No wonder they needed help running this place. I relayed a figure well into the double-digit thousands, and they both sat back and groaned.

"Can't we tone it down some? We can't be taking Christmas away."

Party. Not Christmas, just the party. If these guys really thought their party was the equivalent of Christmas to their employees, they needed to get their egos in check.

"She's never been to our Christmas party before. That's why she thinks we can cancel it," Aiden told his buddy as if "she" weren't sitting right next to him.

"Think about it. We can revisit the subject in a couple of days." I tried to bring the subject to a close. "I've also concluded my payroll and staffing analysis. End of year is not the best time to talk about cutbacks, but they'll have to be made. If revenues stay consistent, we may be able to stretch it to the end of the winter season."

"I can't think about that right now." Gus waved me off.

"In my experience, when cutbacks are necessary, it's best to let the news leak and get people used to the idea before it happens. Often you'll get people out searching for other jobs and quitting before you need to lay them off."

"What if everyone quits?" Aiden argued his worst nightmare. It would mean he'd actually have to do work instead of telling others to do the work.

"We make sure everyone knows which positions are in jeopardy."

"I don't see how you think we can run this place without everyone we have." Gus swiped the knit slouch hat off his head and studied it before putting it on again, despite the thermostat keeping the office warm. He was fully committing to this hipster thing.

My eyes shot toward the desk outside where his office manager "worked." Since I'd already shaken them up with the whole Down with Christmas line, I wouldn't name Gus's personal gofer/office assistant as the easiest staffer to cut and went for the safer option. "You have a human resources director who took five months off and not one thing slipped through the cracks or even fell behind. You're paying her sixty percent more than your two HR coordinators combined, and they managed to do all their work and hers during those five months." Mostly because Tru was exemplary at her job. "Cutting Carly, raising Tru and Mina's salaries for the extra work they'll take on, and placing them as direct reports to Aiden would make a good start at slashing payroll. A few others are in similar redundant positions."

"I don't think we'll get much argument from Carly. She's ready to go, and if we offered a layoff package, she'd have no hard feelings about it." Aiden relayed the surprising fact. Surprising, in that he'd noticed how his employees felt about their jobs. He didn't spend a lot of time with them, preferring to delegate to the department heads.

"Talk about it after the holidays?" Gus effectively dismissed me. He could only handle so much change in one meeting. I'd learned to introduce suggestions in increments.

Back in my office, I made some notes on our discussion. Every meeting inched us closer to profitability, but it felt like a bare-knuckle fight at times. The muscles connecting my neck and shoulders ached. I should book a massage, but the inn's spa needed an overhaul on many fronts. That, too, was not in the budget. Just the thought of all the updates the inn needed added a sharp pain to the dull muscle ache.

My phone beeped a reminder. I had to check the display to remember what it was supposed to remind me, and suddenly, the tightness in my shoulders dissipated. Smiling, I shut down my computer, packed up my satchel, and reached for the binder I brought with me this morning.

Stopping by the second floor on my way out, I didn't have to wait long before Tru looked my way. Whispers gave her a clue something was up. She had every opportunity to covertly request we meet out of eyesight to preserve her popularity, but she grinned and nodded me over.

"Are you leaving early? For the first time in your life, probably." The tease was so out of place in this setting, with every ear in the room straining to listen, but I relished it. Only friends I'd known for years felt comfortable teasing me, but Tru set her own rules, and that was all right by me.

I showed her the binder and tipped my head toward the stairs. No need for everyone on the now silent floor to hear this. Her eyes made a lap around the open space, noticing as heads whipped around to face monitors. Stealthy, they were not. She bit back a smile and stood to follow me.

At the staircase landing, I turned and held out the binder. Her eyes sparkled with curiosity, reaching to take it from my hand. She scanned the first page as I looked on. Her hair, a kaleidoscope of mahogany, russet, and straw-colored strands, was twisted around in back and held in place by two pencils stuck in haphazardly. When she arrived this morning, her hair was hanging free. The makeshift pencil clip was her form of fidgeting, something I noticed during a staff meeting. Instead of taking out her frustration on colleagues as most people would, she reshapes her hair into sexy updos.

She glanced up from reading the first page. "This is so great, Renske. When did you have time to do this?" Her fingers flipped through the laminated pages listing the step-by-step instructions for Penny's file clerk position.

If I wanted to lose every ounce of cool with her, I'd admit to spending my Sunday transcribing everything and organizing the information into concise segments for easy reference. Or how I was late to work this morning after a trip to the only shipping store in town to get the sheets laminated by a wholly unqualified young woman whom I would never entrust with shipping packages even to someplace as close as across the street. Afterward, I spent too much time in the stationary/office supply/gift shop looking through all the available report cover and binder options for just the right one and selected a bright orange— based on her hat and mitten color, I assumed it was a favorite—slim binder. She didn't need to know those activities had been the highlight of my week. It would be too pathetic to admit.

I shrugged, clamping my mouth shut for fear I might say all that in exacting detail because, for some reason, she had a beguiling way of drawing things out of me. Next thing you know, I'd be crying on her shoulder, talking about my childhood.

"Do you have time to give this to her tonight? Over hot chocolate somewhere? If we leave soon, we can catch her before she needs to get a bus."

My eyes blinked and blinked against my will. She was supposed to take the binder to her sister. It's why I risked ruining her reputation by speaking to her amongst her peers. She had to deal with me for business purposes, but she couldn't be seen leaving with Frozen voluntarily. They'd think I was abducting her. Dragging her to my ice cave where I'd periodically turn on my personal snow making machine and blast it in her face.

"You were on your way out, weren't you?" Her eyes dropped to my satchel and the coat over my arm. "Did you have plans you needed to get to right away?"

"You want to go right now?" I tried to give her another out. It was one thing to spend part of the weekend with me away from work for her sister's benefit, quite another to willingly fly in the face of her colleagues' commonly accepted beliefs.

"I got here at seven-thirty this morning. I've put in a full day."

My hands shot up and waved off that concern. "If you don't think it will pressure her to take the job by having me there when you hand this over."

She pressed the binder back into my hands. "You'll hand it over, and you told her you'd do this for her."

I did tell her that. The way Tru reacted to seeing it, though, made me wonder just how many empty promises others had made where her sister was concerned. "Okay, grab your coat and bag. We should be able to catch her before she has to get on a bus."

Her eyebrows fluttered in another butterfly inducing tease. "Why, Renske, ducking out early from work. Who knew you could be so spontaneous and sneaky?"

I could be quite a lot of things if she wanted.

THEIR LOOKS of wonder made this dinner all the more magical. They so freely expressed their enjoyment of everything from the décor to the food to the dining companions. No playing it close to the vest with these three. Pleasure surrounded their every word and gesture. What I thought would be a nice celebratory dinner had turned into an experience not to miss. The last time I'd been out to dinner with someone special was, hmm, two towns ago, three? Shocking. Did I consciously stop dating? Not that this was a date. Certainly not.

"It's just so beautiful," Blythe raved for the tenth time tonight. "Everything."

"My parents took me to a place like this for graduation, but they didn't let me order the cheeseburger I wanted." Sonny looked even more grateful to be able to order a cheeseburger than to be included in our celebration of Blythe's first week at her new job.

Tru's face pinched for just a moment. If my eyes weren't constantly straying back to her, and that beautiful dress and sexy knee-high boots, I wouldn't have caught it. Something about Sonny's parents bothered her.

"But not here?" Blythe asked him. She was wearing a pretty dress, too, and Sonny had on khakis and a dress shirt, which now sported a stain from his beloved cheeseburger.

"Not here," he confirmed. "And I got to eat a cheeseburger."

"He'd have cheeseburgers every day," Blythe told us and laughed with her boyfriend.

"Was it a five-star cheeseburger worthy of the restaurant's rating?" Tru asked him.

He dipped his head, red flushing his cheeks. From what I'd seen, he treated her like she was Blythe's mother, seeking her approval at every turn. "It was the best cheeseburger ever." He turned to me. "Thank you for taking us."

"You're welcome, but we should be thanking and toasting Blythe for getting through her first successful week at the new job." I turned everyone's attention back where it belonged.

"Well done, Blythe," Tru toasted and we all took a sip from our drinks.

"What shall we have for dessert?" I asked them.

Blythe shot her sister a look and gripped Sonny's leg before he could say anything. Tru's hand patted her stomach as she made an exaggerated moan. "Oh, I'm stuffed. Dessert would be too much."

"Dessert is never too much." I wondered if their wide eyes when they first opened the menu had anything to do with not wanting dessert. As the best and newest restaurant in town, food prices were set with wealthy tourists in mind. On Tru's salary, someplace like this would be a once a year special occasion. She must have warned her sister to watch what she ordered when they accepted my invitation. "I'm having dessert. It would be great not to eat alone."

Blythe smiled and nudged Tru. Her eyes landed on mine, a slight shake of her head before she relented and opened the dessert menu. "Let's see what they have."

We placed our orders with the server after much debate over the tasty choices. Blythe continued telling us all about her first week, excitement and relief so evident in everything she shared. She was still nervous about messing up, but with constant assurances from her sister and Penny, she was starting to believe she could learn this job as well as she'd known her last. The full-time hours, salaried position, and benefits provided were icing on the cake.

Tru stood, excusing herself to the bathroom while we waited for dessert. Blythe giggled as she got up, and Tru poked her in the ribs before leaving the table.

"Is that a secret sister thing?" I asked.

Blythe laughed. "It's not a secret. Mom and Dad used to tease her and say her bladder was the size of a thimble."

"Do they say it's bigger now?"

"What?"

"Your parents. Do they say something different about it now?"

She looked away, losing her smile. "No. They died. Four years ago. Car accident. It was awful."

"It is awful," I agreed, swallowing roughly.

"But I have Tru." She regained her smile.

"You're both lucky to have each other." Because not having someone sucked.

"Oh, just fabulous," someone muttered from behind me.

I turned and recognized the marketing director, his gait slightly unsteady, a woman clamped to his elbow to keep him from ramming into tables. Something was wrong with the world when a person was paid so well he could drink to the point of no longer tasting the fabulous food here, but a woman with a decent salary could only enjoy dinners like this for a special treat.

He came closer. "The woman who's holding Christmas hostage."

I turned back to my table, ignoring him. Blythe looked at me with a question creasing her brow. I lifted a stopping hand to keep her from asking anything until he was gone. Engaging drunk guys was never a smart move. Engaging drunk guys already predisposed to hating me, a really stupid move.

"Yeah, typical." He stepped forward and spat out, "Frozen."

"Ooo, I loved that movie," Blythe couldn't help blurting.

I turned back to watch as his eyes went to her, widening when he seemed to notice other people at my table. "This is rich. The only friend you can get to dine with is—"

"One of the most wonderful people in the world?" I interrupted, hoping his drunk state wouldn't make him cruel to innocent bystanders, but not willing to risk it.

"Oh, Renske," Blythe breathed in the same kind of wonder she'd used when describing the restaurant and the food.

"Pathetic," he muttered and lurched past us toward the exit.

"He had too much to drink," Sonny reported, watching the man all the way to the door.

"What did he mean about Christmas?" Blythe asked.

"I recommended the resort skip the Christmas party this year. It's expensive and we're trying to make cutbacks."

"He didn't like that," Sonny reported, which seemed to be his default way of communicating.

Tru walked up to the table just then. "Didn't like what?"

"Skipping the Christmas party," Blythe told her. "A man wasn't very nice to Renske. He was drunk, and Renske thinks I'm a wonderful person."

Tru's eyes shot to mine, questions swirling about. She turned back to her sister and said, "You are a wonderful person."

"So are you, and so is Renske," Blythe said.

"Hey, what about me?" Sonny spoke up, making us all laugh.

"You're dreamy," Blythe told him and leaned in for a quick kiss.

They made a pretty cute couple. It would be interesting to know what the big sister really thought of them. Perhaps I could get her alone for a few minutes to ask her. Perhaps I should make a point of getting her alone to ask her.

13 | TRU

RUMBLINGS SOUNDED THROUGHOUT THE office. Not that they weren't commonplace, but today, they were louder and interspersed with several adjectives for the word "cold." I tuned them out. They didn't know Renske like I did. Not that I knew a lot about her, other than she's considerate and giving, thoughtful and appreciative, reserved and unpretentious. She was in no way cold, yet with her gender, her aloof manner would always be classified as frigid. Presidential elections have been lost on those kinds of false presumptions.

"Winners, us, loser, Frozen."

"Take that, Bitter."

"Screw the Scrooge."

"Would have liked to be in that meeting with Aiden and Icebox."

"Do you think Snowy melts in defeat?"

"Guys!" I raised my voice for the first time in ever at work. Every head turned to me, shocked. "Please stop talking about a coworker that way. It's inappropriate and unkind." Lots of brows raised, but they ceased the insults. "Now, what exactly have we won?"

"The Christmas party is back on. Aiden told his blabbermouth assistant, so everyone knows."

Everyone except me, probably because I'd gotten here early and dove into the performance reviews for the HQ staff and hadn't come up for a breather all day. "And this has to do with Renske, how?"

"She canceled it."

"Because she's a Grinch."

"An icy, subzero Grinch."

"Stop! I'm not kidding," I repeated. Why couldn't they see what a hard worker Renske was? Or how much she cared for the future of their jobs? That every restrictive move she put in place meant they'd get their paychecks on time? "She wouldn't have the power to cancel it. If she made the recommendation, it would have been for financial reasons."

Mina stared open-mouthed at me. "She did cancel it."

I fought the urge to throw back a school yard, "Did not." Once Mina's mind was set, there was no changing it. She used to toss out applicants just because she didn't like their facial hair or sweater choice or how they laughed. They weren't potential dates, they were potential employees. Someone's facial hair or lack thereof wasn't an indicator for job performance. Mina would set her mind, though, and bad facial hair and ugly sweater and cackle laugh would be out of a job.

"She more than canceled it; she told Aiden if they wanted it, they'd have to pay for it themselves," one of the hospitality supervisors spoke up.

"That's not canceling it, then, is it?" I retorted. "As I said, if she told Gus to pay for it personally, she believes the company can't afford it."

"She's obviously wrong if it's back on."

"Or Gus and Aiden ignored her recommendation." And were spending recklessly like they did last year when they forced me to send out an all-staff memo postponing payroll until the opening week's revenues came in.

"What is up with you and Frozen anyway?" Mina barely kept her voice down as everyone else started to settle back into work. "Someone said they saw you talking to her in town the other day."

Oh, the marvels of small towns and their amazingly claustrophobic qualities. "I talk to a lot of people in town. I've run into you many times. Same with a lot of people from work, including Renske."

My intercom buzzed, interrupting her interrogation. Gus summoned Mina and me to his office. We headed up the stairs together, Mina now chattering about the hunky new beer delivery guy she ran into at the bar last weekend. She didn't seem to care that he was ten years her junior or that she was in an eight-month relationship. At least, she'd moved off the Renske rant.

"Ah, good, my A-team. You probably heard, but we've got to get a jump on planning this party," Gus announced as we walked into his office. "Who was that planner we hired last year?"

This was the last thing either of us had time for right now. Our boss was light on work. She could be handling this if only her organizational skills didn't lack organization. "When's the date?"

"This Saturday."

Not only did he go forward with a party we probably couldn't afford, but he moved up the date a week from last year and now we'd have to find a planner with short notice. No doubt that would increase the price.

"I'm so excited." Mina rubbed her hands together. She was thinking about how much fun she always had at these parties, not about all the work we had to do for it, nor about needing to put our normal duties on hold. "What's the budget?"

Gus passed over a sheet of paper. My eyes bulged at the extravagant figure listed there. If Renske advised him not to throw this party, the company couldn't afford it. So instead of prudently following her guideline, he was upping the budget from last year by five figures. He better have some revenue schemes in the works to help pay for this.

"Rad," Mina declared, not caring that it made her sound like a teenager.

"Make sure you get a DJ and a band this year to keep the music going when the band takes a break." Gus shifted his gaze to the window, already distracted after less than a minute.

"Should we maybe bring it down a notch this year? Have the cooks from the lodge do the catering and let one of the employees DJ?"

His eyes came back to mine, narrowing before flicking away. Something was in that look. Something more than annoyance at my defiance telling him he couldn't afford a party. It almost looked like guilt. "Nope, go all out. The employees deserve it."

I wanted to stay and question him more, but he flicked his hand at the door and turned back to the massive window in his office. Skiers and boarders slalomed down the runs in view. We seemed to be as busy as in previous years, but it was hard to tell. Perhaps our financial position was in much better shape than last year and Renske was just overly frugal? Well, not when it came to taking people out to dinner, she wasn't, but that was personal, not professional.

"I'll call the planner and get her started. Oh, and there's this great band I saw in town last week, maybe we can book them. You figure out what the caterers should serve. You're always better at knowing what everyone likes," Mina was ticking off an invisible list in her head. The way she took to these party assignments, she must have been a party planner in her past life. Why she was toiling away in a human resources department escaped me.

"Sure," I murmured, catching sight of Renske in her office as we passed by. "I'll meet you down there. I'm stopping at the restroom."

Mina skipped toward the stairwell, expressing happiness to anyone who'd listen about the upcoming killer party. Instead of turning toward the bathroom, I went to Renske's door and knocked. She looked up and smiled when she saw me. If everyone else could see this smile, they'd never accuse her of being cold.

"Just came from Gus's office. Mina and I have been tasked with party planning."

The smile dimmed, but she waved me inside. "I heard something of the sort earlier today. It doesn't seem like something you should have to deal with."

"All part of the human side of my job."

The grin flared again. "I like that about you."

Warmth flooded my system. She liked something about me. It stood to reason, of course, given how much time we'd spent together recently, but it was nice to have it confirmed. I liked so many things about her as well.

"Shall I put you down as the first RSVP?" I fluttered my eyebrows. Employees rarely RSVP'd, usually just stopped by my desk and asked if they could bring more than the plus one everyone was allowed.

Her head shook, some of the mussed strands sliding further out of place. "No."

My face fell and my stomach followed. I'd been kidding about the formality of RSVPing to a company shindig, and she declined going to the party entirely. Come to think of it, she'd missed the company picnic in the summer, the Labor Day picnic, and the Halloween bash. Did she not like parties? I assumed she wasn't seeing anyone since she didn't show up at dinner the other night with someone, nor had she mentioned having a partner. Perhaps going alone to parties intimated her.

"There will be a bunch of us going solo if that's holding you back. Not that you don't have or couldn't get a date. Of course, you could. It's just if you...sorry, entirely inappropriate workplace conversation." I could feel heat burning my cheeks. What was I doing talking to her about how easily she could get a date? I worked in HR for pity's sake.

"Tru," she started, helping me out of the embarrassing hole I was digging myself into. "I don't think I should partake in the benefits of a party I recommended not happen."

"Oh." I understood. I didn't want to because I really wanted to see her at the party. I wanted other people to see her at the party, see her as my sister and I have seen her.

"I'm sure you'll do a great job putting it together." Her lips pulled into a smile. "Like everything else you do."

She was incredibly sweet, and it was infuriating to know I was the only one around here who recognized it.

14 | TRU

EXTRAVAGANCE EVERYWHERE I LOOKED.
This year's extra ten grand for the Christmas party could be
seen and tasted and swilled all over. It surpassed any of the
others thrown in the past. Not that it made the employees
enjoy it any better. As was usually the case, my coworkers
loved the buildup to the party, but once they got here, it
became more of an obligation than something to enjoy. All
the personal differences we ignore at work were spotlighted
when forced to act socially. Finding out someone's wife was
a boorish alcoholic or someone's husband was a vapid
narcissist rarely helps smooth over coworker relations.

Mina and I had been here two hours, helping the party
planner with last minute arrangements and greeting people
as they came. The shuttle drivers were working overtime to
bring people out to the lodge and take them home to
accommodate the generous open bar. Gus and Aiden gave
speeches, then every director and most managers made
speeches. I was speeched out, partied out, talked out. My

122 | LYNN GALLI

coworker relationships were always good, but seeing them getting progressively sloshed and uninhibited never helped to endear them further. In previous years, they'd get two drink tickets and had to purchase the rest of their drinks, which kept them from getting to the dancing-with-lampshades-on-heads stage. Tonight was a different story, and we were only two hours in.

"Where's your date?" Mina asked as she sidled up to me. Her hands clung to her boyfriend's muscular arm. Their saga was well known among the mountain staff. They'd been together eight months but only exclusive for three. This distinction was made after Mina found out he'd been seeing someone else for the first five months of their relationship. He was a personal trainer at the gym in town and could make anyone feel guilty about not working out just by looking at his impressive shape.

"Are you enjoying yourselves?"

"Rad party," the trainer commented, his free hand clutching a craft beer.

"We worked hard to make it so," Mina bragged. Her blue eyes searched the area around us. "You brought someone, didn't you?"

"No." I usually didn't. These people were easy enough to get along with, until they were sloshed. Then they were mostly obnoxious. Certainly not something I'd want a date exposed to.

"Did you check out the new store owner over at the village? The one selling holiday trinkets. She's cute, a little older, but cute. You should go for it."

She's twenty-five years older, newly divorced, enjoying the freedom and the lovely tourists, not at all looking to be tied down again, but sure, she's cute.

"You're a lesbian?" personal trainer guy asked. "Man, I know loads of women down at the gym if you're looking."

I held back a laugh. The population of this small ski town didn't have loads of anything, let alone women who'd date other women. His offer was sweet, though. "Thanks, but I'm good." Or I would be if a certain someone was at this party.

"She kills with those dimples," Mina told him, tipping her chin at me.

My dimples flashed them both when I smiled at her comment. It wasn't like I purposely smiled a certain way to get them to show. They showed whenever I smiled. Either I go through life as a stone-faced grump, or a dimpled, unintentional temptress. Trainer guy laughed when he saw the dimples and laughed again when Mina tugged on his arm to get them moving back into the party.

My gaze made a round trip around the lodge. Gus was busy telling the same stories he told every year, his wife by his side, acting as if she'd never heard the stories. Aiden joined them with a curvy young woman I'd spotted in the grocery store before. I thought about going over to make excuses to leave and thought better of it. They were already tipsy. They'd never remember I left early.

Outside, I easily found my car in the sparse lot. Nearly everyone was taking advantage of the designed-driver shuttles. I got in and started the engine, cursing the blast of cold air that blew from the vents. The car was seven years old and starting to show it. The heat didn't come on as quickly or as strong, and clearing the fog from the windshield took one long, frigid minute. I shouldn't complain, though. It got me where I needed to go every day. In a couple of years, I could splurge for a better snow car. Blythe hadn't stopped talking about Renske's seat warmers. She didn't take note of the luxury brand, the fine leather seats, the amazing entertainment console, or the many other premium features. All she cared about were seat warmers and wanted me to treat myself to a new car with a winter package. Encouraged me to use some of her trust fund, which we'd set up with our parents' insurance payout and their remaining savings. I couldn't bring myself to do that. The money in her trust had a purpose. Blythe was ten years younger, and even with a shorter life expectancy, she could outlive me. When I die, she'll need extra help with the things I do for her. Help that would come at a cost. I wouldn't take from that need just for a minor luxury like seat warmers.

With a frozen behind and slowly warming air blowing near my face, I eased the car forward as soon as the windshield defrosted. No snow tonight, which was a blessing. No one was leaving as early as I was either. I should be home sooner than most of my colleagues could finish their third drinks.

At the stop sign near town, I checked my mirrors. No cars in any direction. Without letting myself chicken out, I grabbed my phone and punched in Renske's number. She could be having her own party or out on a date or settled into her jammies for a night in. I blew out several breaths, which were no longer visible in the warming interior. The phone rang and rang, my nerves twisted and twisted. I should hang up. This was stupid. Just because I wanted her to be gay didn't mean she was. She must know about me, everyone at work did. But she could easily be a straight woman perfectly cool with having lesbian friends and not constantly bringing the subject up as so many straight friends did. Either way, she was not answering, and therefore, not interested tonight. Hanging up now.

"Hello?" the phone said.

"Oh, hey, Renske, it's—"

"Tru, hello. How's the party?"

"I left early."

"Not to your liking?" She didn't sound annoyed at my use of her personal number on a Saturday night. In fact, her tone sounded receptive, exactly what I'd been hoping for.

"It was the same as every other year." Except more expensive.

"Do you leave early every year?" Now her tone was playful, and my nerves turned into swirly goodness.

"Often, yes." I made a hopeful turn on the road, away from my house. "You wouldn't want to grab a drink, would you? If you're free, I mean. You might be on your way out or settled in for—"

"I'd love to," she interrupted. "Where?"

I gave her a suggestion, ready to give another, but she went for the first. Within five minutes I was parked near the pub and on my way in. To a possible—please, let me be right about this—date.

THE BAR WASN'T POPULAR for the college crowd who came up for the weekend to ski, nor was it the choice for all the hearty, local types. It was sophisticated but not pretentious, frequented mainly by the professionals in town.

She was ten minutes behind me, striding through the door without any sign of the nerves I was feeling. My eyes strolled over her freshly outfitted form. Like me, she was in wool trousers and ankle boots. Unlike me, she wore a teal green silk turtleneck that slicked down over her breasts and torso like a downhiller clinging to the slopes for more speed. It peeked out from under one of her fabulous coats, a fitted trench in creamy white. She had at least five other stylish overcoats, not counting her ski parka. They were of various lengths and materials, all signature pieces for her outfits. This one was wool, hit below the knee with a wide belt, doubled back and tied to keep out of the way. As much as I admired it, I couldn't wait for her to slip it off.

My strolling gaze finally ended at her eyes, which flared slightly when she must have recognized my appraisal. Smokey shadow brought out the golden color of her eyes. Her lips shined with clear lip gloss, and the cold outside pinked her cheeks. Her hair was groomed with paste, which made the blond strands appear not-all-the-way dry. When it was mussed, as it was by the end of nearly every day, strands fell over the tips of her ears and along her temples. Tonight, though, she'd redone her hair and changed from a casual Saturday outfit to meet me. A promising development, for sure.

"Hello." She stopped at the two-person booth I'd chosen, slipping out of her trench and hanging it on the hook of the seatback.

"Hi. I'm glad you were free tonight."

As she took her seat, her eyes slid down over me. She looked pleased with the perusal, settling on my dangly earrings for a few extra seconds. "It's the best invitation I've had in...well, since your Thanksgiving."

"My Thanksgiving?" I teased, lifting my fingers into a small wave to catch our server's attention.

"Hey, Tru, good to see you." Jeanie was a former classmate who married her high school sweetheart, got pregnant—not in that order—and now had three other kids. She worked here to get out of the madness of her house some nights. We were friendly, but with nothing in common, not friends, exactly like in high school.

I returned her greeting, but her eyes had gone to Renske, brow raised in question. She'd been nosey in high school, too. I made introductions or we'd never be able to place our drink orders.

"How long have you lived here?" Renske asked as soon as Jeanie left.

"Born here. I went away to college and for a few years after."

"Do you know most everyone in town?"

"Surprisingly, no. Only about twenty-five percent of the natives stay in town or come back later in life."

"Did you know you'd be one of the twenty-five percent?"

"No, I actually took a job in San Diego at the headquarters of a hotel chain." I thought back to accepting that position rather than another closer to home. "I missed my sister and parents, but I needed my independence, too. Then, Blythe graduated from high school and had a hard time adjusting to her part-time job and having all the people she knew off away at college. I asked to transfer to the chain's local hotel to offer a little more stability and familiarity for my sister. Then, our parents died, and so now, this is home."

She nodded, her eyes never looking away as so many others did when touching on uncomfortable subjects. "Your sister mentioned your parents. I'm sorry you had to go through that."

"It was a tough time. My sister was nineteen and dependent on them. I'd had the luxury of ten extra years with them and some independence. She was devastated, her first experience with grief. She'd never even had a pet die. Nothing to ease her into the process." I lifted my shoulders, feeling some of that helplessness overpower me again. "Like I said, a really hard, horrible time."

"I can imagine." Her hand reached across the small table and landed on mine. Smooth and strong, when it squeezed mine, I felt it everywhere.

We took sips of our drinks, letting the low murmurs in the bar fill the space between us. I had so many questions for her, but the urgency to know everything right now wavered. It wasn't as important as just enjoying her company.

"You were in Jackson Hole before this?" I asked.

"I was. Nice company, excellent skiing, but not many challenges when it came to my job. Everything ran pretty smoothly there."

"Unlike here," I muttered and got a soft laugh from her side of the table. "Let's get back to the 'my Thanksgiving' thing. Do you not celebrate holidays?"

She waved her long-fingered hand through the air. "I usually work holidays, but my mother was from the Netherlands, so Thanksgiving was never a thing for us."

Was. Damn. "Is she no longer with us?"

"No." Succinct, toneless.

"I'm sorry to hear that." Over the years, I'd heard many people attempt to express sympathy. It never helped. Only others who'd lost a parent early in life could possibly understand. "It's never fair, is it? Was it a car accident like with my parents?"

Her eyes searched mine, intensity and conflict clouding them. "She was murdered."

I swallowed hard. "Oh, my God. That's horrible."

"It was." She looked away, breath quickening. "Looked like a mugging, but the detectives found out it was a murder for hire. My mother wasn't the target. The man she was seeing at the time had a business partner who wanted him gone. It was just bad timing for my mom to be with him that night."

My hands made the trek across the table to grasp hers. "When did this happen?"

"I was fifteen, away at a ski race. We were supposed to leave that afternoon, but the team's plane got delayed by weather. My teammates were ready to quit over missing Christmas morning at home."

"It was Christmas Eve?" I couldn't stop my voice from rising in dismay. Her mother was murdered on a day billions of people eagerly anticipated. She must go through an exhausting range of emotions every Christmas season.

She turned her gaze back and nodded. "Made the investigation get off to a slow start, but they did their jobs, found the guy responsible. Not that it really matters in the end."

No, probably not. Her mother was still gone. "Was your father a comfort like Blythe was for me?"

She scoffed softly. "My parents were still married. He didn't know about the affair. So, no, he wasn't eager to comfort, not that he was that kind of father to begin with."

This kept getting worse and worse. How had she managed to get through this without going insane or getting so angry she'd want to shred everyone in sight? "Was he there for you later, at least?"

"I filed for emancipation when I turned sixteen. It was best for both of us."

I wanted to gather her up and hug her for days. She might have had many hugs over her lifetime, but not one of mine. I'd gotten lots of practice with my champion hugger sister. I wanted very much to share that skill with Renske. Give her something tangible. Words weren't enough. I gazed at her, wanting to make that move, knowing it would be awkward given our seating chart, but feeling the compulsion all the same. Since I wasn't sure how she'd react to that compulsion, we continued to regard each other from across the table.

"I'm happy you're here," I finally said. Our silent consideration of each other said more than conversation could in these circumstances.

Her lips pulled into a brief smile, acknowledging and appreciating the conversation shift. "Me, too."

We stayed for another drink, moving onto lighter topics. As I'd hoped, we had no problem conversing. Even more than at work, her intelligence flowed through her words and expressions. A sharp wit and ardor magnified her already attractive personality. I was no longer merely enticed, I'd skipped over crushing, and landed on outright enthralled.

Outside, the street was quiet. Nearby storefronts were closed. Only the streetlights kept the area bright. My breath plumed out in front of me. I had one arm through my pea coat, reaching back to fit the other, and found Renske guiding it into place for me. She tugged and righted the coat onto my shoulder. Her hands arranged the collar before she stepped aside, nodding her head in the direction of her car. Mine was a few spaces beyond.

"That was fun," I said as we approached her car. The spotless silver metallic paint of her Mercedes gleamed in the streetlight. I was glad her car was parked closer, or I'd be embarrassed by how desperately my car needed a wash.

"It was," she agreed, turning to face me at the driver's door.

"My good luck to find you free tonight. We should do this again, don't you think? Have a drink or dinner or we could go skiing on a weekend?" My mouth kept talking as my eyes kept bouncing between her eyes and lips. She'd intrigued me with that mouth all night. Every word she spoke, every smile she gave, every sip she took mesmerized. More, I needed more. What did it feel like, what did it taste like, did she kiss in little nibbles or long, hungry draws? "I know year-end is a busy time for you, so after the new year works. If that's something you—mmmrfph!"

She smothered my words with a bruising kiss. Her hands gripped my lapels and swung me around to press up against her immaculate car. The chill of the metal against my back contrasted with the fire her mouth was igniting inside me. Every answer about that mouth overwhelmed me at once, delicate softness, gentle suction, heavenly pressure, tangy and sweet, insistent and yielding, agile and carefree. No other kiss had sparked such all-consuming sensations. I was now ruined for future kisses. Wrecked, busted, bankrupt. Her kiss would forever be at the top.

Her mouth gentled over mine, finishing with two light smooches. She pulled back, looking into my eyes. A smile flickered. "I really hope that's what you were working up to."

My breath left me in a rush. I let out a laugh, the air clouding for an instant between us. "Not very well. It might have taken another few minutes of awkward suggestions."

"Nothing awkward, all good suggestions." She chuckled and reached to lay her cool fingers on my cheek.

"You don't know how many more I had. At some point I might have suggested curling."

"I might like curling."

"I want to know that. I want to know everything you like."

She sucked in a breath, her eyes moving from the stroke of her fingers on my cheek up to my eyes. Dark brown rimmed the amber color. I wanted to spend hours studying her eyes, all her features. Crazy to think we'd been merely colleagues a few weeks ago. Colleagues with little interaction, and now I hankered for so much more.

"Dinner, to start. We can try curling some other time."

"Tomorrow night? Wait, no, Sonny's parents are having a dinner. Monday night?" My craving spoke for me when my mind should have been screaming, "Pull up, pull up. You're sounding desperate."

She watched me, probably reading my mind or mirroring my mind, but then, her glorious mouth smiled and came near again. One soft kiss, one clear message.

"Monday," she confirmed and turned to open her car door. She didn't move inside. Her wait at the open car door finally getting through to me as I hurried a few spaces away to my car. Only when I ducked into mine, did she get into hers.

In years past, company parties had always been enjoyable, but nothing compared to this particular after-party. I was certain nothing ever would.

16 | TRU

"EPIC PARTY, BRO." A guy in marketing high-fived another guy in IT.

Hour five of the party recap, complete with painful descriptions of various people upchucking in places I didn't want to think about and embarrassing behavior along with sexual indiscretions between, until that point, unacquainted coworkers on the seasonal staff. Mina had criticized my choice to hold back two grand from the budget for a cleaning crew, but she wasn't surprised or unhappy when their invoice came in at nearly that amount. For more than one reason, I was really glad to have skipped out early. I missed a lot of the crazy behavior and would have missed out on a crazy good date.

My gaze wandered the floor. Employees had bloodshot eyes, as if the sleep they might have gotten last night didn't make up for all the sleep they'd missed on Saturday's debauchery. They dragged in this morning, slumping into their chairs, barely managing to log in. Within an hour and two cups of coffee, they'd come back to the land of the living and started in on their Monday morning quarterbacking of the annual holiday party. Phones were passed around, showing pictures from the party. If any work had taken place all morning and now into the afternoon, I missed it. As suspected, no one noticed my early departure. Several others told me they'd left an hour or so after me when things started getting really crazy. The seasonal youngsters had taken over the dance floor and the bar and the world, it seemed. Many of the headquarters staff got out before bodily fluids became visible.

Their fond recollections didn't come close to the good time I'd had after leaving the party. Just thinking about it brought on the warm tinglies. Oh, and that kiss, high-five worthy, shout from the rooftops worthy, hurry down to the chapel worthy.

Not even the dinner with Sonny's overly formal and protective parents last night dimmed my mood. Normally they could make even someone as upbeat as me gnash my teeth. It wasn't just how much they impeded Sonny's development by doing absolutely everything for him, but they really didn't approve of him being in a relationship. They didn't have anything against Blythe. In fact, they'd always liked Blythe, but they had a difficult time admitting their son was not a boy any longer. Not that I liked to think of my kid sister as a sexual being, but for parents it was even more difficult. For parents of differently abled kids, nearly impossible. But their roadblocks hadn't been enough to stop the friends who were also roommates become a couple. Now, they felt obligated to invite my sister and me to dinner occasionally to appear as if they supported the relationship.

"Shh, Frozen's on deck."

"Can you believe Brisk didn't show up?"

"She was too busy stealing Christmas from Whoville."

"Iceberg sinks parties."

"Igloo could have at least brought some ice for our drinks."

"Surprised Frosty hasn't suggested tearing down the inn and building a hotel made of ice."

"That reminds me of where Aiden's latest squeeze said they'd be spending the holidays." And that started a gossip session about Aiden and his holiday exploits. At least it got them to stop talking about Renske.

My head swiveled round and spotted Renske heading for the marketing director's office. A small sigh escaped as I watched her going over something on her tablet. Today she wore slacks and a silk shirt over a camisole. I wondered if she'd paired it with her silver cashmere overcoat wrap or her maroon double-breasted thigh length trench. Either would look good with the pinstriped charcoal trousers and pale blue shirt. The left side of her hairstyle had broken free of the product and dipped forward, brushing her cheek. My fingertips prickled with wanting. I could almost feel them sweep through to push the strands into place.

She clapped the cover over her tablet and strode out of the office, coming toward me. Unsuccessfully, I tried hiding the ear to ear grin. She looked serious, as she usually did, no matching smile, which wasn't surprising. Her head nodded once at me, a polite smile, and then she looked at Mina and gave her the exact same treatment before sweeping past to my boss's office. My stomach churned at her offhand greeting. Okay, so she was a professional. She was reserved, especially at work. It wasn't like the kiss hadn't meant anything to her. Her rapid breaths and dilated pupils and flushed neck told me just how much the kiss had meant to her. And it wasn't like she didn't remember we had a date tonight. I couldn't expect her to sweep onto the floor, drag me to a stand, so she could dip me into a smoldering kiss in front of everyone. That wouldn't suit either of us, but a little secret smile would have been nice.

"What's that about?" Mina asked, her eyes following Renske into Carly's office.

"What?" A blush battled with the sudden onset of nerves that I might have blown the evening out of proportion. Just because she enjoyed our kiss didn't mean she was as over the moon for me as I was getting to be for her.

"Frozen smiled at me."

"Stop calling her that," I said automatically. She wasn't Frozen. That much I knew for certain. "She smiles. Get to know her and she smiles."

Mina's hands came up in defense. "Jeez, chill. I was just saying she seems like she's in a good mood today. Maybe she had a better time not going to the Christmas party."

I pressed a hand to my cheeks, happy not to feel them burning. I hope Renske had a better time not going to the Christmas party, but I wouldn't make that announcement now. She wasn't wearing the silly grin I was, but others might still recognize a shift in her demeanor.

Renske poked her head out of the office to call us inside. I forced myself not to stare too long as she and Carly talked about moving the headquarters' staff performance reviews to the off season. She just managed to make my insides jump for joy again, this time for professional reasons. Even Mina gushed about the wonderful idea.

We headed back to our desks, happy to focus on more imperative tasks during the busy season. As I turned away from Mina, something brushed against my elbow. A fleeting touch. So slight, I barely felt it. Then, a whiff of white tea wafted past my nose, and I turned to find Renske standing near. My eyes found hers, and what her office-appropriate expression didn't say, those eyes did.

"Good day?" she asked. Not even her calm politeness could quiet the thrill her touch brought.

"So far," I replied, more successful at shutting down the goofy smile this time.

Her eyes made a quick check of the room before her fingers came forward and swiped once more along my elbow. "Thanks for the help in there." She turned her head and said, "You, too, Mina. Hope this helps keep your department focused on the important things during the high season."

"It should. Thanks for suggesting it," Mina confirmed, disbelief at our good fortune still apparent in her glassy eyes.

"Right, then," Renske said, her eyes dropping to my lips briefly before she moved past our desks and toward the landing.

"Can you believe that? What's gotten into her?"

I turned away, not wanting her to read the hope on my face. If I had a little to do with what Mina perceived as a change in Renske, I'd take the win. Perhaps Mina could get everyone to start calling her Thaw instead of Frozen.

17 | TRU

RENSKE WAS EVEN MORE beautifully attired tonight in a boat neck cashmere sweater, fitted slacks, and a belted cape that somehow didn't look costumey on her. If I tried to rock that cape, I'd resemble someone trying to dress up as Supergirl. When she arrived, she leaned down to kiss my cheek before taking her seat across from me. Still slightly reserved, but not at all the vision of the staid professional she was in the office earlier.

Throughout dinner, more and more of her personality came to light. In the office, she was unruffled. With my sister, she was unsparing. Tonight, she was confident and serene. I was entranced, wanting to know more and feel more and have more with her. Everything I'd always wanted from a date.

"They what?" Her rigid expression just before our plates were cleared should have worried me. Instead, I wanted to drag her across the table and lay a big smooch on her wonderfully outraged lips.

We'd been talking about Blythe, which led to probing into how I felt about her boyfriend, which further led to discussion of his parents. "Well, not last night, and certainly not in front of their son or my sister."

"They better not. Those absolute swine!" She looked ready to take up a sword and storm their castle. My insides started quaking with how protective she was. "Sterilization? Unbelievable. Who are they to think they could decide that?"

No one would accuse her of being detached right now. She was infuriated, as if Blythe meant as much to her as she did to me. For four years, I'd been alone in dealing with helping prepare my sister for the world without much assistance from anyone. Occasional chats with her overworked social worker helped a bit, but it was nice to have someone stand in Blythe's corner for Blythe alone.

"They couldn't even bring themselves to talk about condoms with their son, let alone sex. They didn't want to be responsible for a baby if Blythe got pregnant." Which would be difficult since our parents gave her the sex and birth control talk when she was a teenager. Later when Blythe was ready, we visited her doctor to choose the best option for her.

"And their sexist asses didn't think a vasectomy would be easier? Assholes. Do not let me meet them." Her fierce gaze shot to the window as if expecting Sonny's parents to be lurking outside.

I remembered feeling the same anger and disgust talking to his parents. It made me appreciate mine even more. They encouraged everything we did and wanted. Sonny's parents obviously preferred to discourage rather than support his aspirations. My dad might have come to blows with Sonny's dad if he'd been alive during that discussion. As it was, I stopped just short of calling them barbarians for the suggestion. The dinners had been strained ever since.

"Don't hold it against Sonny. He lets his parents dictate a lot, but he has put his foot down about some things, like moving out and dating Blythe. He's a devoted friend and boyfriend, but he needs his parent's approval and support. I've seen him take great strides since he's moved out, but he didn't have the same benefits Blythe did."

"Like an older sister who adored her and taught her everything parents often have a hard time teaching their kids?"

"We were lucky all around. Our parents worked with her to think independently. Sonny's parents are codependent. They need Sonny to need them. At least he's got a part-time job now, so he's getting more independent by the day."

"He seems like a nice guy."

"He is. Can't stand that he's my sister's boyfriend, but I guess she'd have to get one sooner or later, and it might as well be a devoted guy like Sonny."

"Is she as protective of you with girlfriends?"

I blushed. It was technically only our second date, but I was ready to jump right to the girlfriend stage with Renske. "She's always encouraging. I try to be as well, but I worry in private."

"Maybe she does, too."

"Can I interest you in dessert, ladies?" Our waiter stood at the table without either of us noticing when he arrived.

Renske opened her mouth, her head shaking, but remembered and glanced at me first. I was ready to get out of here, too. After paying the check, we made our way outside. I turned to ask where she parked and felt my heart squeeze tight. She was staring at me with open hunger. Flames of lust grew from the sparks I'd been feeling throughout dinner into a roaring wildfire.

"Drinks or coffee at my place?" I wanted some privacy with her, something more than a kiss up against her car, an amazing kiss, but still only one kiss.

"Mine's closer." She gestured down the block, reaching out to take my hand. Cool skin slid against my palm as our fingers locked together. She glanced down at our joined hands. For a moment, we just stood there, connected. All the promise of the evening stood before us. Her lips twitched, the hint of a smile, then she tugged us into motion.

An inch of snow gathered on the sidewalks, broken by a few footprints from diners leaving the restaurant. Her place was close, but she led us to my car for the quick drive. Either she was worried it might be towed from in front of the restaurant or she didn't want our date shoes to get soaked on the walk.

Minutes later, we stepped out of my car in front of an end unit in her sleek, modern townhouse complex. She took me up a flight of stairs and unlocked her front door. Lights came on automatically as she disarmed her alarm.

"Nice place." I looked around the airy, yet severe space. Lots of white and sharp edges. Only a gorgeous cello standing in the far corner of the living room gave the room any character among the pristine fixtures and furniture.

"It works for me." She swept a hand toward the couch. "Would you like coffee or a drink?"

"Whatever you're having."

She smiled and turned toward the kitchen, a stockpile of stainless steel. Taking a step, she stopped and turned back. Her eyes latched onto mine, and in the next moment, she was moving forward. To me. My arms were suddenly up and around her shoulders, fingers shooting through the short hair at the back of her head. She moved her gaze over my face, ending on my lips. I tipped forward to capture her mouth. The little noise she made set off a series of pleasurable explosions in my chest. Her arms came around my back to bring our bodies together. She tilted her head, sliding her lips across mine. My tongue skated along her top lip, teasing before pushing inside. Hers was right there, accepting and encouraging.

I moaned and shifted my legs, thrusting my thigh between hers. I wanted to climb inside her, tangle and jumble our limbs and bodies so neither of us knew where we started or ended.

She ripped her head away, her eyes burning with desire. "We should stop. Now. Or I won't be able to."

My breath came out in gasps. My legs were still entwined with hers, hips pressed together, arms still locked around her neck. The last remaining part of my brain still able to think clearly knew she was right. We should stop. We were colleagues. It was only our second date. There was still so much about her I didn't know. We could be romantically disastrous together, and then have to go on working in close proximity.

"We should, but that's not what I want. Do you?"

She brought a hand up to trace my lips. "I don't ever want to stop."

Every part of me clenched with her admission. I glanced over her shoulder to a hallway beyond the living room.

"One thing," she said, planting a soft kiss on the corner of my mouth and trailing her lips across my cheek to my earlobe. "I don't want to ask after we've already been intimate. It would be embarrassing then."

I blinked, processing. What could she want to ask me that might be embarrassing tomorrow? "This sounds ominous."

She laughed and my insides jiggled with her levity. "Is your name short for something? Trudy? Gertrude? Astrud? Truckee?"

I barked a laugh at her guesses. "Truckee? Really? For a girl?"

She took my mouth with hers, silencing my laugh. "Can you see why it would be embarrassing to ask after we've slept together?"

"Truly."

"So, you do understand. Did I nail it on the head, Truckee?"

I laughed again, loving this new devilish side to her. My head shook in answer to her question. "Nice to meet you, Renske. I'm Truly."

"Truly," she whispered, awe in her soft tone. Then she jerked back. "Wait. You're Truly Daring?"

I tilted my head and shrugged. "My parents thought it would be clever. They learned their lesson by the time Blythe came along."

"It fits." She leaned close again. Her lips nibbled along my jaw as her hands roamed up my sides, thumbs stopping below my breasts. "Did I interrupt the mood?"

"Not a chance." I turned to capture her mouth.

She dropped a hand to mine, pulling out of my kiss to drag us toward the hallway. We race walked toward the last door on the right. Her bedroom was as stark as her living room, not that I had time to study it. As soon as we crossed the threshold, she gripped my shoulders and maneuvered me onto the bed. Her knee came down next to my thighs as her fingers searched out the zipper of my dress. She pulled the material forward, stripping me to the waist. Her eyes prowled over my torso. Heat licked everywhere she looked.

I pushed my hands under her sweater, taking it up and off. The black satin bra contrasted sharply with her glorious pale skin. She stepped into a stand to kick off her boots and shuck her slacks, suddenly in a hurry. Her hands came to my waist, tugging at the dress. I raised my hips to help.

"Beautiful," she murmured.

"Perfection," I admitted as my eyes memorized her toned physique.

Her hand pressed against my shoulder, encouraging me to lie back. Her face loomed over mine, eyes giving away her desire again. She dipped down, lips covering mine in a searing kiss.

I clutched at her sides to pull her down on top of me. She moaned, I hissed. Hot skin, velvety smooth tantalized mine. Scorching lips pulled and plucked and plundered my mouth. Adept fingers released my bra and discarded my panties and took her own off. Finally, she settled over me, bare skin to bare skin. Beautiful amber eyes burning and lusting and wanting so much.

My hands skated up from her waist, stopping below her breasts. I looked into her eyes as I cupped her breasts and thumbed her nipples.

Her eyes slammed shut. "Mmm, yes."

She shifted her weight to one elbow, freeing a hand to drift up my body. Fingertips grazed my breast, then flipped over and backed along the same path. She stretched her index finger to swipe over my nipple, spiking it to a point. I moaned and pushed into her hand. Her head swooped down, mouth sucking my nipple inside, tongue batting and lashing.

My hips rolled up against hers. She stiffened over me, pulling her head away and pressing her hand against the bed. Her mouth came back to mine as her hips began a slow grind. Hot, slick, titillating friction. I met every roll of her hips with my own. My hands helped coax her rhythm.

Our mouths met again, hungry kisses devoured. She wedged a hand between us, sliding down, down, my hips bucking up, up. Finally, her fingers found my excitement. This time, she hissed, and I moaned.

My eyes found hers, words weren't necessary. We felt them with every rock of our bodies, every graze of our hands. "I need." "I want." "Let me." "Touch me."

She dipped her fingers into my cleft, circling, swiping, tapping. My hips jolted off the bed. Sparks sizzled through my nervous system. Overload was just around the corner.

I gained the last ounce of my control and pushed a hand between us. She lifted up just enough to allow me room but continued rocking with me. My hand found her plump, wet center. I extended my index and middle fingers to rub her swollen clit. She groaned and rocked her hips harder.

Her fingers ceased circling and slid down, probing my opening. She paused and looked into my eyes, then slowly pushed inside. I let out a moan. She pulled back and added a second finger, filling me. "You feel so good."

"Need you," I said between heaving breaths.

She nodded once and pumped her hips faster. I slid my finger into place, and on the next surge of her hips, drove inside her. She murmured something, dropping her lips to my ear. Hot breath spilled out, engulfing my senses. I fitted my thumb against her clit and drew circles while continuing to thrust up into her. She met every thrust with one of her own. When her thumb grazed my clit, I seized up and shouted her name, shuddering through my convulsions. She stilled her fingers but kept rocking through my climax, drawing it out to a full minute until I was wrung out, wiped, and completely sated.

She stared down at me, eyes wandering over my face and chest. Satisfaction animated her expression. "Good?"

"Mm-hmm," I managed, growing more and more aware of the sensations outside my body again.

She lay against my side, having denied herself to slake my needs. Energy poured back into me, and I turned on my side to press her onto her back. She stared up at me, a smile playing on those talented lips. I brought my mouth to her neck, kissing down her throat to her chest and onto her breast. My lips found a nipple, nipping the tight bud. She squirmed beneath me, needing more. I dropped my hand to her stomach and skimmed it down over her mound to cup her. Squeezing once, I slipped through her folds. No warning this time, my fingers plunged inside, thumb circling her clit. She released a breathy sound and started panting with every pump of my fingers. Her intense gaze lost focus as the sounds grew more audible. Hands shot out to grip my ass, increasing our tempo. She sucked in two sharp breaths and let them out in a long climactic groan. Pulsations grabbed at my fingers as her body spasmed and shook beneath me.

"Amazing," she whispered once her body calmed. She slung an arm around my waist, using the last of her energy.

"Spectacular," I agreed and leaned down to kiss her.

"I wouldn't hate doing that again."

I laughed, happiness bursting inside me. A month ago, I was still a little scared of this entirely composed woman. Looking at her now, icy-blond hair in disarray, amber eyes sparkling with renewed lust, and naked body flushed from orgasm, nothing about her was composed or aloof. She was pure passion and fire, about as far away from frozen as a person could get. And I felt lucky to share in the benefits.

MY BODY STILL BUZZED and hummed and quivered. It had nothing to do with a lack of sleep. Needless to say, I hated having to leave for work this morning. Waking up spooned against Renske's naked chest, I never wanted to move. When Renske's alarm went off, she was just as tempted to play hooky from work, but her will power was impressive. She remembered a budget meeting she had with Gus and Aiden, something they'd pushed off repeatedly until she got them to agree to this make-or-break date. She couldn't miss it. I admired her dedication, even if it cut short my slinky, steamy, salacious morning-after.

"You'll never believe it," Mina announced loudly, not caring if she disturbed anyone while we were trying to work.

"On the phone," someone hissed, but Mina gave him a meaningful stare, and he took the hint to hang up the phone.

Mina looked like she might burst with her news. "Frozen got fired."

WHAT! A shout sounded inside my head. *What?* Lowercase shout, but no less stunning.

"Really, Wintry?"

"Are you sure it was Frigid?"

"No way. Polar got the boot?"

"Did Gus get frostbite when he kicked her out the door?"

"What did Arctic do to get canned?"

"You'll seriously never believe it." Mina couldn't have looked more thrilled if she were being paid to tell this story.

"Is this for certain?" I interjected, knowing how Mina loved to repeat gossip.

"For sure. Heard it from Nadia." Mina mentioned Gus's gofer/office manager. "You know she's got nothing to do when she's in the office. So, she started using the intercom to listen in on meetings in Gus's office. This time she pulled out her phone to record it."

A fireable offense, but that didn't seem to be the action that got someone fired today.

"So Frozen goes in—"

"Renske," I interrupted. The least she could do was call Renske by her name.

Mina shot her eyes to me, a moment of guilt making her pause. "Right, Renske goes in to talk about some of Gus's recent purchases and the Christmas party spending."

"What purchases?" someone from marketing asked.

"He bought another shuttle, two more snow blowers, and six snowmobiles to start offering trail rides."

Two outfits in town already offered snowmobile adventures for tourists. Unless Gus was planning to let guests take the machines on the slopes—a really, really bad idea—the other outfits had much better trails. What was he thinking? Which was probably the question Renske asked.

"Anyway." Mina leaned in, the crowd around our cubicles growing by the second. "She starts telling him why that was a bad idea, and you know how Gus doesn't like being told he made a mistake. Then she harps on the party spending, and she didn't even go to the damn thing. But I'll give props to her on one thing. She called him out on how men are paid more than women around here. I'm glad there aren't any men in HR. I'd be pissed if I found out I was paid less than a guy in my position."

If I was capable of biting someone's head off, I'd do it now. Pay equality wasn't only about equal pay for the same positions, but equal pay for similar positions. As in, did that dufus in marketing get paid more than Mina and I? I wouldn't mind if Harold in operations did. He had ten more years' experience and a master's degree. But the marketing dufus was two years out of college and barely managed to contribute anything.

"She wanted to give us raises?" a female member of the marketing department asked. Perhaps she knew for certain the marketing dufus made more than she did.

"That doesn't sound like Icebox."

"Maybe Bitter's not so icy."

About damn time some of these idiots acknowledged that. But where was the outrage for one of our colleagues being fired for voicing her opinion?

"As I was saying," Mina sounded out each word to grab everyone's attention again. "She brings up a loan she said wasn't on the books or not in the right place on the books, like he was purposely hiding it or something. That's when Gus started shouting and Nadia cut off the intercom in case one of them came out, but she could still hear him fire Renske."

"Damn."

"Holy moly."

"Rad."

"Did she storm out of there crying?"

Mina shook her head. "Nope, apparently, she walked out, calm as can be, even said goodbye to Nadia as if she was just going back to her office. But Nadia saw her leave the floor with her coat and briefcase soon after."

So, maybe she wasn't really fired but told to take the rest of the day off to let everyone settle down.

"Unbelievable. So, she's really gone. No more wintry winds blowing through the office."

"That's unfair," I spoke up. Something burned in my chest at the thought of Gus shouting at Renske. She worked so hard for his business. Cared more about its welfare than he did these days. Was I really the only one who could see this? "None of you have tried to get to know her. Gus and

Aiden make her play the bad guy when you want something the business can't afford, and you blame her. She's not the bad guy, and those names you call her are cruel."

Mina looked suitably guilty, considering Renske just did our department a huge favor yesterday. "Hey, I gave her props for the gender pay thingy."

I swallowed my rising panic. Our working relationship was such a nice piece of our relationship as a whole. Anytime I wanted to get a glimpse of her or hear her voice, she was never more than a floor away. I had to know if this was more than a rumor.

Sneaking out after the gossip circle disbanded, I took the steps two at a time. I didn't need to step off the third-floor landing. Her office lights were out, which meant she wasn't there. Downstairs, I peeked out the front entrance to the parking lot and couldn't find her car. So, she had left already. Hopefully it was a difference of opinion that prompted the early exit, not something permanent. Gus didn't usually overreact to things, but he had been more stressed lately.

I tried her phone, leaving a message when she didn't pick up. She could still be driving home and might not feel like talking right now. Maybe needed to cool down and digest the meeting a bit. Knowing that didn't make it any easier to go back to my cube to get some work done.

After work, I didn't wait to drive home before calling Renske again. No answer and no response to the text I sent. She didn't seem the type to cry into her cornflakes while binge-watching daytime talk shows, but I also couldn't imagine her being open to a drop by if she had been fired. Mina tried to get Aiden to confirm the rumor, but he blew it off and went skiing for the rest of his workday.

I battled my desire to swing by her townhouse and went home instead. Blythe was there, likely spending the night as she did two or three times a week. She wasn't always up to dealing with the conflict that often comes with roommates. Gideon proved particularly difficult to reason with at times. His inability to recognize social cues meant he didn't understand why his roommates got mad when he stayed up all night watching horror movies or playing video games. Jolie was a neat freak and got upset when her roommates didn't clean as obsessively as she did. And Sonny forgot to do many of the chores assigned to him because he'd never been expected to pitch in at his family home. When it got too much for Blythe, she'd come home to spend the night in her room. Sometimes she brought Jolie with her, but thankfully, she hadn't brought Sonny home for a sleepover yet. I knew it was just a matter of time, but I could live in my imaginary innocent sister world a little longer.

"Hi, Tru." Her bright smiling face greeted me the moment I stepped through the door. "Fun day?"

"Hi, sis." I dropped my purse onto the console table and hung up my coat. "Not a great day, no. How was yours?"

"Penny needed me to help make copies for her big case and asked me if I could pick up lunch 'cause her assistant was out sick today. I got to order whatever I wanted, and we all ate together in the big conference room." She grinned broadly, another successful day at work knocked out. Then, her brow furrowed, remembering my initial response before I distracted her with a question. "What happened for you?"

"I'm not sure. Renske might have had a really bad day, but I can't get a hold of her."

"She came by the office today. I forgot!" She looked pleasantly surprised, not at all troubled by forgetting something.

"She did?" It made sense she'd seek out her friend for some consoling if any part of the rumor was true. I just wished she would have turned to me as well.

"Yep. Before we closed, but Penny was super busy with her case, so she just stopped by the file room to say hello."

"Did she say anything about her day at work?"

"Nope. She was her usual self."

I wasn't, even before all this kicked off at work. Last night was still spinning my mind. The feel of her skin against mine. Her skilled touch and whispered words. My mind jumbled with images and remembered sensations. Add this thing with work, and I couldn't think straight.

When my phone buzzed, I shot up from the couch and rushed to the counter. A text from Renske. Finally. And she wanted to stop by. I could feel the spin cycle in my head slowing to its end.

Fifteen minutes later, I let her in the house. She looked worn out, her hair had broken free of its sleek style. Strands brushed against her ears and temples and stuck up in back where she must have run her hand repeatedly. Still, she had a smile for me, and it grew much bigger when I opened my arms. She stepped into them, stiff but not shying away. I kissed her cheek and would have kissed her mouth if Blythe hadn't called out for her. She barely made it out of my arms before Blythe had her wrapped into one of her champion hugs.

"Good to see you again," Renske told her as she accepted the hug without any hesitation. "You were pretty buried in work when I stopped by."

"I know. I told Tru." Blythe pulled back and looked up at her. "What happened at work? Tru said it was a bad day?"

She smiled down at my sister, who still had her hands on Renske's shoulders even as she tried to turn and get us moving into the living room. She allowed my sister to pull her inside and place her on the sofa. Blythe took the spot next to her. Sometimes, my sister's eagerness was cute. Tonight, I wished she'd taken an extra hour to get home. I wanted nothing more than to be sitting next to Renske and holding her hand. Her downtrodden demeanor said Mina's accounting of the meeting must be true.

"There was a disagreement about the finances. The boss didn't appreciate it and asked me to leave."

"Permanently?" I had to ask.

Her head nodded. "I've never been fired before. Doesn't feel so good."

"But you're the queen of numbers," Blythe stated simply.

Renske chuckled, releasing some of the tension she came here with. "He's going to find another queen, I guess."

I moved to kneel in front of her, reaching to grasp one of her hands. "Do you know what you're going to do?"

"Not yet. Still in shock."

"Come work with Penny," my sister decided on the spot. Simple solutions were her specialty.

Renske turned a grateful smile her way. "They're a bit too lawyerly over there for my taste, but thanks for the suggestion. I'll figure something out."

"Have a sleepover with us tonight," Blythe told her.

Renske's eyes shot to mine, some of the heat from last night making them dance, but the hardship of her day kept them in check. "Thanks, but I'm beat. I'm going to head home. I just wanted to see a couple of friendly faces after my day."

"How about a piece of pie to go? That'll help cheer her up, don't you think, Blythe?"

"Yes!" she exclaimed and darted into the kitchen for the leftover pie we always had in the fridge.

I lifted my hand to cradle Renske's cheek. "I'm sorry this happened."

"So am I. And my day started out so great." She leaned her head down to touch mine.

"So did mine," I told her. "You know, Gus can be a hothead. He'll probably beg you to come back before the end of the week."

She closed her eyes and breathed in. "Doubt it. I called him out on a couple of things he can't come back from."

I coaxed her arms around my neck and tilted up to brush my lips against hers. I wanted to ask her to stay tonight, or always. Not to look at other ski resorts, even if working at resorts has always been her calling. We were just starting out, and yet, already so settled. This morning, our first morning-after, there'd been no awkwardness. No shyness, no regret that we'd moved too fast. If she looked at other resorts, I'd lose her. Other mountains were too far away to commute, and far enough to make having a long-distance relationship difficult. We could try it for months until our every weekend visits turned to every other weekend, and then, once a month, and finally, fizzled out. Tonight, wasn't the night to say anything. Tonight, she needed support and warmth and to know that people cared about her horrible day. I really wanted her to stay over, but she was used to being alone. Understanding that would have to do for now.

She moved in for another kiss, lingering longer than my lip brush. She sighed against my mouth and pushed back, ready to stand. I understood. She wasn't used to the kind of affection and caring my sister and I took for granted. Something I would work hard at changing for her.

19 | TRU

GUS DIDN'T ACKNOWLEDGE FIRING
Renske until Friday. Well, not so much acknowledged firing as acknowledged she no longer worked for the resort. Made it sound like it was her choice. And he wasn't telling everyone, just those of us in human resources.

My own feelings on the matter aside, I wanted to throttle my ADD big boss for flicking the information out and then moving on to another subject. Like getting rid of the person most fiscally responsible in the company was no big deal. Certainly not as exciting as needing to hire several snowmobile operators to start a new ride service.

Renske had more propriety than the CEO of the company. Whatever disapproval she expressed about his financial decisions, she wouldn't blab about them. Not even to me. She was still smarting from being let go, and her mind had been preoccupied every time we talked. Tonight, I hoped to break through that preoccupation when we got together. If she wanted encouragement to start looking for other positions in town, I was prepared with insight on several local companies. If she wanted support or a sympathetic ear, I'd be there for her. She'd gone through so much of her life alone. I would do whatever she needed to make her understand she wouldn't have to handle this on her own.

"You'll get right on those hires, then?" Gus turned back from the window where he was admiring the new snowmobiles lined up behind one of the supply outbuildings.

"Certainly," Carly agreed.

"Great, great." He glanced out the window again. "I'd also like you to look into layoff options for a few employees. I think we're a tad overstaffed. Might have gotten a little ahead of myself this year, so see what might be a decent offering if we have to lay some people off."

My eyebrows hiked up. Were we nearing another payroll freeze? I was good with money, had an emergency savings account as well as a decent retirement plan, but I didn't have a lot of discretionary income. After paying my expenses and helping Blythe with some of hers, not much was left. Thankfully, Blythe now had full benefits, which gave my finances a lot more breathing room. Still, any delay in getting paid was a hardship, and not just for me.

"How many are we talking about?" Carly's tone was cautious. She had a wealthy husband, so it wasn't finances making her nervous. She wanted to avoid dealing with all the anger thrown at our department when we'd had to share the news of the payroll freeze last year.

"Nothing's been decided. A dozen or so, maybe more. We've got several part-timers that aren't necessary, just convenient."

Except the part-timers didn't cost us thirty percent more for benefits. Part-timers weren't the problem. Laying off the people who actually did the work wouldn't help us. Laying off the people who managed the work would be a better choice, but I wasn't the CEO.

"When would the layoffs happen?" I asked.

"After the holidays. Come up with what we can offer, how we'd go about telling them, if there are outplacement options for them, things like that."

This was far more than he'd ever wanted us to do for outgoing employees. Something seemed off here, but I couldn't pinpoint what.

Mina crowded close as we headed back downstairs. It was her signal that she wanted to talk without the boss hearing. She waited at my cube until Carly shut her office door, then she tugged on my arm to take us into the bathroom. She checked under the stalls to make sure we were alone before she started talking.

"What the hell was that? Is he going to hold back our salaries again? Toss everyone out?"

"Let's not jump to any conclusions yet. He asked us to look into it. Could be revenues are higher than expected, and he calls it off like he did last year."

Her head nodded repeatedly as she exhaled. "Yeah, okay, yes. That would be good. I can't afford to lose this job. I just bought a new car, and I've been saving up for my wedding."

I blinked in confusion. "Did I miss something? You're getting married?"

"Not yet, but I think he's going to propose at Christmas. He's like that. So romantic."

Or smart but economical. Combine an expensive gift like an engagement ring with a major gift-giving occasion, and rather than two gifts on separate days, one gift on one day. "That's wonderful," I said as if it really happened and wasn't just a hope in her mind.

"Thanks, I can't wait for Christmas morning."

I'll bet. I had my own hope for Christmas morning, or afternoon, since I was stuck working the morning. I didn't know if I'd even see Renske that day, let alone be able to spend time with her and exchange gifts. She wasn't a big fan of holidays, but Christmas must be extremely difficult for her. She hadn't spoken a lot more about losing her mother, but she did say Christmas day had never been the same since.

"We'd better get back."

"You really think he's just looking at options?" Mina's anxiety peeked through her prior happiness.

"I wish I could say for sure, but I really don't know. You heard what Nadia said about his meeting with Renske. She must have been calling him out on something financial." I knew that much for certain. Which part of the financials, I didn't know.

"You talk to her outside of work, don't you? Has she said anything?"

"Yes, but she wouldn't disclose something like that. She has integrity."

"Did you ask her? She seemed to like you."

My brow went up in surprise. I didn't think Mina noticed anything other than what she perceived as coldness from Renske. "She does, and I like her. You would, too, if you got to know her. She won't say anything about it, though. She had as much confidentiality attached to her department as we do in ours."

"I know she's incredibly smart, but I hope she's wrong about her financial concerns."

I doubted Renske was wrong about anything, but I wouldn't worry Mina.

It was difficult to get through the rest of the day. Felt like Mina and I were carrying around a huge secret that could harm many of our colleagues. Staying positive, I took Gus at his word, assuming he'd only lay off the most recent hires, and only if the revenues fell short of his expectations.

Leaving the office helped lift my mood. I had the weekend to digest what I hoped would be nothing more than another of Gus's passing ideas. I also had a date with Renske tonight. If all went well, we'd have a better understanding of where we stood with each other. If we still worked together, things wouldn't be up in the air.

Obviously, we were attracted to each other, liked each other, enjoyed spending time together. But was it enough for her?

She opened her front door, a beautiful, welcoming smile on her face. We were having dinner at her place. Her sterile, zero personality, ultra-chic townhouse. I should have asked her back to my house, but I was so happy to be getting together with her I agreed to her suggestion. Not that I didn't like her place, it just didn't fit the Renske I knew. It fit the Renske everyone at work thought they knew.

After dinner, we took our wine glasses and sat close on the stiff but showroom-worthy couch. A fire crackled in the gas fireplace opposite. Her hand roamed from my arm, up to my shoulder, and now fingertips stroked my neck. The contrast between how good her hand felt and the discomfort of her couch kept me from completely relaxing into this.

"You comfortable?" The huskiness in her voice added to the shivers already running through me.

"Yes."

"Really?" Her head tipped forward, lips planting several nibbles on my mouth. "This couch is dreadful, isn't it?"

I chuckled and captured her mouth, no more teasing nibbles. My tongue swept along her lower lip. Hers surged forward to tease mine into her mouth. We dueled for the enjoyment, not dominance. It seemed like such a simple thing, kissing for enjoyment, not escalation to something more. Pleasure, not authority. Every kiss should be like this. They all should have been, but until Renske, I'd been kidding myself.

"Are you giving me a hint for your Christmas present?" I spoke while brushing my lips over her chin and down her neck.

She stiffened, and I felt the tightness everywhere we touched. Then, she was pressing me into the nonexistent cushioning of the sofa backrest. Her mouth skated over my jaw, clearly trying to distract me from her moment of tension.

"I was kidding," I said gently. "Presents aren't necessary." Even if I really wished they were. I liked giving and receiving gifts. My sister and I gave each other little presents all the time. For Christmas, we could spend an hour unwrapping all the little gifts, a lot of them handmade. I wanted nothing more than for Renske to join us, with or without presents.

"Is that right?"

Her teasing tone should have pleased me, but I couldn't help feeling it was covering her discomfort with either the holidays, or gift-giving, or spending the holidays with me. We hadn't really discussed her plans since she'd been fired. I was already in so deep with her after only two real dates. If I went any deeper and she left town for another resort, I'd be devastated. Even with my usual positive outlook, I couldn't see coming back from the damage she could cause to my heart.

"Something's up," she guessed, pulling back and studying me. "Christmas is a thing for you, isn't it?"

"It's not that." Partly that, but not the real concern. "I've been wondering what you'll do next. If you're going to have to leave."

Her eyes darted away as her chest expanded with a cleansing breath. "I've been looking at options. I'd like to stay, obviously. You're a wonderful motivator for that."

Shivers zipped along my nervous system. "I know you have to do what's necessary for your career."

"But?" She tipped my chin up to lock eyes with mine.

"I know we're still so new, but I'm already hooked on you." Surprise registered on her features. I was a little surprised myself. Not that I was hooked so soon, but that I'd admit it so soon. "I want to spend more time with you. A lot more time with you. I'd be crushed if you got hired on at another resort. I should be noble about this, but I'd regret not asking you to place more consideration on opportunities close by."

Her lips tugged into a smile. "Noble, eh? I think you're perfectly noble. I'm glad you told me."

She swooped in for a kiss, a distracting kiss, one that led to us standing and retiring to her bedroom. It wasn't until the next day I realized she still hadn't told me about any plans she was considering.

IF ONE MORE PERSON stopped by my desk to ask what this all-staff meeting was about, I might do something really uncharacteristic like raise my voice or mimic some of the more negative guesses going around. I was already on edge with the project Gus set us on, and now I needed to rejumble the Christmas day work schedule to accommodate the employees who threatened to quit for religious reasons if they were forced to work. My workload felt like it was crushing me.

It didn't help that Renske left town a few days ago for some mysterious meetings—not interviews, she assured me—with nothing more than a promise to try to make it back by Friday, also known as Christmas. It was selfish of me to want to spend the holiday with her. Christmas Eve and Christmas day brought reminders laced with sadness and loneliness for her. I still didn't know how she managed under the weight of her crushing grief. Having to grow up instantly with no support from her remaining parent, it was no wonder she'd rather forget the holidays existed. Still, I really wanted to spend the day with her. Blythe would be equally crestfallen. She already thought of Renske as family, and that was before I told her Renske and I were now dating.

At least something wonderful came from her impromptu journey. Renske, stoic, professional, reserved Renske, was incredibly skilled at phone sex. Heat blotched my cheeks as I thought about the turn our phone call took last night. I shouldn't have been surprised; she was a seriously talented lover. It made sense she'd be able to describe sexy scenarios just as well, but knowing that and experiencing it were two very different pleasures. It also served as yet another distraction from pinning her down about those meetings and whether or not I'd see her on Christmas day.

Mina interrupted my thoughts by tugging on my arm. I glanced up to see a mass of people moving toward the stairwell for the meeting no one knew anything about. We merged with the flow down to the first floor and outside through the covered walkway to the lodge. We joined the mountain staff as they crowded into the space around the fireplace as all the tables in the cafeteria were already taken. Our boss was up front with the rest of the senior staff and motioned Mina and I to stand close by. We had to push our way through, prompting more questions from everyone we passed.

Gus and Aiden came in from the kitchen, and the racket in the room grew louder at their appearance. Only Gus climbing up onto a table had any effect, dropping the noise level to something manageable.

His gaze traveled around the room. "There's no sense in dragging this out. We have some unfortunate news. Despite our efforts to increase revenues from the new ideas we've tried this year, the setbacks we had over the last two years have caught up to us."

Concerned muttering and grumbles broke through the quiet of the room. People nudged me from behind, leaning forward to whisper in my ear. Like I knew what he was talking about any more than they did.

Aiden climbed up next to him and patted the air to get everyone to settle down. "If you'll remember, one of the lifts broke down a couple years ago and needed replacing. Last year was the lodge remodel. We took out loans to cover both, and snow conditions last year cut into our profits."

A sinking feeling took hold the more they spoke. Taking into consideration Gus's special research project last week, I could now guess exactly what they were trying to say in their distracted way. The directors all appeared to know what was going on, so they must have been told earlier. Mina gave me a meaningful look, alarm sharpening her usually delicate features.

Aiden stepped forward again. Gus tried to wave him off, but they ended up having a frenzied discussion until people started shouting questions at them. Gus looked shocked at the raised voices. His self-involved nature wouldn't have anticipated this kind of response.

"Listen, we've done everything we can. It's not certain, but it looks like the bank could start foreclosure proceedings soon. Honestly, we've tried everything to bring in more income, but nothing worked out like we hoped. We're appealing to investors to see if we can find a buyer, but we don't have much time."

Now everyone seemed to understand what he was saying. The mountain, his business, the one where we all worked was going out of business. We were all out of a job. Damn, was this what prompted Renske's exit? She must have called him out on his irresponsible fiscal management. Then, there was how much he'd spent on that stupid party. He could have used those funds to stave off foreclosure proceedings. But no, like a man about to go to prison for the rest of his life, he tossed all of his cash reserves into a blowout party.

"We're closing?" someone shouted.

"What the hell, Gus?"

"Damn, dude. What are we supposed to do?"

"We understand your concern," Aiden said as if all this amounted to was nothing more than taking ham sandwiches off the cafeteria menu. "We've asked our HR department to compile job listings around town and at other resorts. They're going to help you with your applications and prepare you for the interviews."

No, we weren't. That wasn't at all what they'd asked us to do.

"We're probably a month away from a foreclosure notice. That should take another thirty days, so you've got a job for another two months at least." Gus had the nerve to smile at this, as if having a job for only two more months was any less devastating than not having a job at all.

"We do have some good news, though," Aiden interjected and gestured for Gus to continue.

"We'll be offering a two-week layoff package for anyone who stays on through the foreclosure. And we've decided to close the resort on Christmas day so no one has to work the holiday, but you'll get paid for the day. It's our gift to you."

More exclamations sounded from the crowd. Gus and Aiden swatted them away with cheery "the good news is" retorts. My sinking feeling dragged me under completely. I wanted to throttle them for their carefree attitude in managing this place. I didn't bother thinking about my predicament and how I couldn't be without a job for long and the awful prospect of going back to the hotel chain I'd worked for. My focus was on everyone else here. Our resort was the biggest employer in town; we wouldn't find enough jobs for everyone. I wasn't worried about the seasonals. They could all go to other mountains in the west. The HQ staff would be harder to place.

Gus and Aiden swept out of the room, leaving the other executives to try to calm their own groups. Everyone looked to Carly eventually, and she clearly wanted to teleport into outer space to avoid having to assure everyone our department could help them.

I wanted to call Renske. Hear her voice. Let it soothe me. Calm and assure me. Even though she'd gotten fired from the same company now going out of business, she'd be a comfort to me. If she were like a couple of my ex-girlfriends, she would snort and say, "Good. Serves those assholes right." She wouldn't do that. She'd express sorrow about the loss of jobs for me and everyone else because she knew what that feels like and because she tried to stop it from happening.

It would be hours before I could make that call. Looking at this mob, many, many hours to quiet them and assure them we were doing whatever we could to help them find new jobs. But I'd call her, and she'd make my day better. I was certain of that.

SOFT KNOCKING ON MY bedroom door woke me Christmas morning. Prying my eyes open, I checked the clock. Six-thirty. After the long, long day and night at work yesterday, I was too tired to even sigh.

"Tru?" My sister's attempt at a whisper was laughable. She didn't want to wake me up, but it was Christmas morning and she wanted us to be up. She'd gotten over the disappointment of not spending any part of today with her boyfriend, who was at his grandparents' house for the week, as quickly as she got over every disappointment she faced. It helped her to know she'd be sleeping in her room at home and waking up to spend the whole day with me, unlike other Christmases when I had to work eight to ten hours. "Tru? Come on, it's Christmas!"

I laughed, which was her invitation to burst through the door and pounce onto my bed. She wrapped me in a full body hug. "Merry Christmas, my favorite sister."

She giggled and squeezed me tight. "Merry Christmas, my favorite *only* sister."

"Did Santa come last night?" I stared into her bespectacled eyes.

She sighed and wiggled in my arms. "We have to get up and see."

"Honey, can I shower first? Maybe have some coffee and breakfast?"

"Tru!" she whined as she did every year when I faked delaying the opening of presents.

"One stocking gift first." I gave in as I always did. It was our routine.

"Let's go." She slithered out of my arms and scooched to the end of the bed and onto her feet.

I took a little longer to roll to the edge and get upright. Blythe grabbed my robe and helped me into it to get us moving. Thankfully, her frantic state kept me from feeling too dejected over Renske not being here with us. Earlier this week, she told me she hoped to get a seat on a flight home tonight. After I called to tell her about Gus's meeting, she said she'd fly standby if she had to.

The blue spruce scent of the tree clung to the living room as we made our way downstairs in our jammies and robes. Blythe's eyes widened at the extra presents I laid out last night before dropping into my coma sleep. Several of the presents were gifted from Santa, which always made Blythe giggle when she opened them.

Stockings knit by our mother hung from the mantel. I turned on the fireplace, thankful I'd converted from wood to gas when we downsized from our parents' house and bought this two-bedroom place. The heat blasted out, warming the air around us. Blythe turned on the Christmas tree lights and sat cross-legged on the floor, eyeing all of the presents. We'd lost all of our grandparents, but our parents' brothers and sisters usually made a point of sending Blythe a present. She was special to everyone in the family and better than Facebook for catching everyone up. Our cousins would call her first whenever they needed confirmation of some family rumor. My parents used to call her the family dispatcher, and Blythe loved the role. Several of them would send little knickknack gifts with their Christmas cards each year.

"Ooo, I don't know which one to pick," Blythe eyed the four small wrapped gifts she pulled from the oversized stocking.

I loved how hard the decision was for her. She never took anything for granted. It didn't matter that she'd have them all open after breakfast in less than an hour; she agonized over choosing one now.

"How about this one?" I held up the smallest cylindrical packet, ends twisted and tied with yarn.

She grinned and reached for it, examining the tag Santa made for her and the snowman wrapping paper. Within seconds she ripped it open and was screeching at the Miss Piggy lanyard inside. A four-dollar gift and she couldn't be more excited. When she first started working at Penny's, she needed a lanyard for the security access card and only boring black ones could be found in town. I had to special order one featuring her favorite Muppet.

"Oh, thank you, Tru, I mean, Santa." She looked skyward, like Santa might still be on the rooftop. "I love Miss Piggy."

"Santa knows."

She pointed to one of my stocking gifts. "That's a good one."

"This one?" I picked up a different one and she gripped my hand and pushed it at the one she pointed to. Carefully, I unwrapped the gift because it drove Blythe crazy how long I took. Inside was a colorful business card holder made of pottery. For Christmas last year, I'd given her ten trips to the pottery painting store in town. She liked crafting and spent hours painting and fussing over different pieces of pottery. This was one of her best. Two skiers set against a familiar looking mountain with a ski lift running to the top. My eyes misted. Only my sister would take part of the gift I'd given her and turn it into a gift for me the next year.

"It's beautiful, Blythe. You're so talented. Thank you." I tipped forward and wrapped her in my arms.

"Do you really like it? The instructor said it was good, but I don't think I made the skiers very good."

"They're amazing. It's going to look so great on my desk. Thank you." I stood and placed the holder on the kitchen island, prominently displayed. A few friends and two sets of neighbors usually dropped by at some point every Christmas. I'd want them to ooo and ahh over it. "Shower time. I'll start the coffee, and you think about what you want for breakfast while you're getting dressed."

"Okay." She hopped up and squeezed me around the middle before darting upstairs.

I glanced at my phone, pushing aside the disappointment of no texts waiting for me. If Renske had managed to get on a plane earlier than expected, she probably would have texted. I shouldn't be disappointed. Yesterday was a tough day for her. Since she was in New York, she planned to visit her mom's grave. She didn't sound mournful when we spoke before she made the trip, but it could have hit her hard once she got there. I felt powerless several states away, but I think I was able to give her some comfort.

After showering and getting dressed, I sat on my bed for a moment and held a silent discussion with my parents. I knew they were looking out for us, happy we were together, pleased to see us both successful, proud of us both. My mom loved Christmas, so it had always been an all-out holiday for us. My sister and I tried to carry on that tradition, but it was important to remember how much we missed without our parents here to share it with us.

"Thinking about Mom and Daddy?" Blythe came in and sat next to me.

I slipped an arm around her. "I was. They'd be so proud of us and happy we're having a wonderful Christmas."

"I know." Her voice cracked slightly as she buried her face in my neck. "Miss them."

"Me, too."

"We have each other," Blythe spoke our usual chant.

"That's right."

"And I have Sonny, and you have Renske. And we both have friends and other family. We have everything."

I swallowed the boulder sized lump in my throat. My sister had somehow taken over the role of positive Polly in our family. Usually it was me reminding her of all we had when she got morose about missing our parents.

"We'll feel better with full bellies." She patted her stomach and stood, pulling me up with her. "Let's do French toast. I'm so glad you don't have to work today."

So was I, even if it meant I probably wouldn't be working at the same place in a couple of months. After the disaster of a meeting the day before yesterday, Gus and Aiden called our department in to give us answers to some of the questions we kept hearing. They admitted there was a slim chance they could find investors in time to buy out the property and keep it running. If the bank foreclosed, it would be months, possibly years, before they sold it and the resort was up and running again. Too long for anyone to hope to hold out for a job. In between checking jobsites and the websites of many businesses in town, I sent an email to my old supervisor at the hotel. I wasn't sure if I was hoping she'd respond with a "welcome back" or a "nothing's open right now" email. The idea of going back to the more boring job didn't appeal, but it was better than no job at all.

Breakfast was a joint effort and speedily consumed. We did a quick cleanup, and then Blythe was ready to rip into the rest of her presents. I snapped several pictures of her after she opened each one. She always included them in the email or text she'd send to everyone in the family when she thanked them.

"Bet that's the Wilsons next door," Blythe guessed when the doorbell rang. "They're going to love the peanut brittle we made everyone this year."

I opened the door and felt my heart start into a gallop. Not the Wilsons, but Renske, looking impossibly fresh and beautiful, despite traveling across the country overnight and into the morning. I surged into her arms, pressing my lips to her neck and kissing my way up to her mouth.

"Well, hello to you, too." She sounded amused after accepting my kiss. "You look beautiful."

"You look amazing. I'm so happy you're here."

She glanced away, the hardship of yesterday appeared on her face for a moment. "I'm happy to be here with you."

"Renske!" Blythe shouted and started into a run that ended in a slide and into Renske's open arms. "Merry Christmas. Tru said you might not make it, but I knew you would."

Renske's eyes watered as she bent to clutch her just as hard. "Merry Christmas, Blythe. Was Santa good to you this year?"

Blythe laughed and nodded, tugging on Renske's hand to bring her inside. She delayed the effort, turning to pick up the bags she'd brought with her. Blythe helped her carry one of the bags, eager to get into the living room and back to her gift opening position.

Renske laid a hand on my shoulder, turning me back to face her. She leaned forward and kissed me, soft, full of every kind of sexy promise. "I missed you."

"I missed you, too. I'm eager to hear all about your trip."

She smiled and butterflies broke free in my stomach. This wasn't the smile of someone who'd landed a job several states away from her new relationship. "I want to hear about what's happening at work for you, but there are more important things to do right now."

We joined Blythe on the floor near the tree. She'd already dug out the presents we had for Renske and placed the gifts Renske brought beside them. Renske looked a little shell-shocked at how to proceed, which saddened me. This couldn't be the first Christmas she'd spent with a girlfriend or friend in the past. Yet, her expression seemed to be saying that.

"You have to open your stocking gift first," Blythe told her. "We didn't have time to make a stocking for you this year, but this would have been in it. Santa left it on the mantel for you."

Renske laughed and reached for the box Blythe was holding out. "How did Santa know I'd be here?"

"Santa knows everything," Blythe told her and winked at me.

She unwrapped the silvery paper to reveal a plain box. Flipping open the top, she reached in and pulled out a small snow globe depicting two windmills and a colorful tulip field. I'd searched and searched online for something that wouldn't be too touristy when Blythe decided this was what we should get Renske for the stocking gift.

"It's Holland," Blythe exclaimed.

Renske's eyes misted again as she nodded. "Yes, I see. It's beautiful. Reminds me of everything I miss about the Netherlands."

"Tru said you went to school there?"

"Yes, boarding school for many years. I loved it there. This is wonderful. Thank you." She blinked away the moisture in her eyes and shook the snow globe to make little flower petals and snowflakes rain down over the windmills.

"Should Tru open her present?" Blythe asked.

"Why don't you open yours first?" I told her, knowing she was itching to get her hands on the gift next to her.

Blythe did her careful examination, asked if she could shake the box, and made some guesses. All the while, Renske's smile grew wider as she leaned closer, slipping her arm around me. I couldn't think of anything better than sharing this moment with her.

By the time Blythe pulled an expensive pair of rose gold headphones out of their packaging, she was squealing with delight. She had them on her head instantly, dislodging the arms of her glasses and not caring.

"They're noise canceling as well as regular headphones," Renske told her. She picked up the packaging box and showed her several features. "When I stopped by your office last week, the scanner and both printers were going. People crowded around the file boxes on the other desk. Lots of noise. These will let you tune all that out when you want a little peace and quiet in your space. Or if you want to listen to your music or a book, we'll get them synced to your phone."

I turned a grateful look her way. She'd listened to every worry I had about Blythe's working conditions. Too much distraction could overwhelm my sister. Multitasking was difficult for her. Her new job had plenty of both, and there were days when Blythe had to step outside to call me for a calming moment. We'd talked to Penny about how Blythe could best do her work, and it helped, but these headphones would provide a way for her to shut everyone else out when things got too much. Renske somehow picked this up about Blythe after only one office visit. Then, she cared enough to find a solution. I couldn't wait to thank her properly.

"They're so pretty," Blythe murmured, running her hands over the stylish design. "Thank you, Renske. I love them." She tipped forward and hugged her.

"You're welcome. I'm glad you like them."

We spent the next ten minutes opening the rest of the presents. Renske fawned over the forest green pea coat from me and put it on to model for us. I tried to hide my shock at the designer bag she'd gotten for me. We needed to have a discussion about dollar limits on presents for our next gift-giving holiday, but it wouldn't stop me from enjoying this incredible bag.

When she opened Blythe's gift, a beanie hat knit by my sister in a bright gold color that had taken Blythe an hour in the store to choose, she didn't notice the four dropped stitches and the slightly askew cable knit pattern. She raved about its shape and pattern and color and popped it right onto her perfectly styled hair to show how much she liked it. I felt my heart squeeze almost painfully. Warmth pulsed through my limbs, and my vision wavered.

This wasn't new anymore. It wasn't the start of something. This was it for me. I shouldn't feel that confident about our relationship yet. I shouldn't feel that certain about someone as guarded as Renske. But I did. I knew I'd fallen for her. And I knew, without doubt, I'd love her for the rest of my life.

Okay, so...yeah. She better be good with that.

TRU FLIPPED pancakes she made from scratch. From scratch, with non-boxed ingredients. It wasn't like this was my first made-from-scratch breakfast or even my first hot breakfast cooked by a hot woman. It was, however, my first time realizing I never wanted to miss another hot breakfast made from scratch by a hot woman. This hot woman, specifically, not just any hot woman. I'd be happy with cold breakfast or dashing out the door with a cup of coffee as long as it was with this hot woman.

"Should we wake Blythe?" I glanced toward the staircase.

"She sleeps in on weekends." Tru turned with a grin. "Plus, she was up extra early yesterday to see what Santa brought."

I wasn't sure about spending the night with Blythe staying over, but I was sure about not wanting to go home after the day we'd had together. If she let me, I'd stay the whole weekend. That awareness stunned me. I liked being alone, never suffered from loneliness, and yet, I was here after an afternoon and evening and night together and didn't want to flee.

I poured our coffee and offered again to help with breakfast. Tru waved it off, brandishing the pancake pan as she slid the pancakes onto a serving dish. She gestured to the pantry, and I retrieved the syrup, then joined her at the table.

She turned and lifted a hand to tuck loose strands of hair behind my ear. "It's nice having you here."

"Nice being here," I confirmed and pushed into her hand, craving more contact. More everything, really.

"You didn't finish telling me about your trip last night."

"You distracted me." I swooped in for a kiss before she took her first bite.

She hummed against my mouth, savoring the kiss. The sound kickstarted my arousal, or maybe it just flared the arousal which had been my constant companion since first wanting to kiss her. "It was a great distraction." She pulled back and picked up a fork. "Tell me how it went."

I thought about what I'd told her so far. How much I'd never told anyone. Why I didn't tell them. What would happen if they found out. What had happened without anyone knowing the full extent. As I was trying to figure out how much to reveal, Tru turned and flashed her sweet smile, dimples drawing me in, and I knew I could tell her anything.

"First, I should tell you one of the reasons I filed for emancipation as a minor."

She sat back, mouth opening, then closing. I'd stunned her with my non-sequitur, but she processed quickly, turning to face me with her full attention. "I'd like to know."

I pulled in a breath, amazed such a simple claim could give me the assurance I needed. Coming from someone so genuine, I believed she did want to know and not just about this. She wanted to know anything and everything I could tell her about myself. More importantly, I wanted to know the same about her.

I thought about where to start and dove in. "My parents were both career focused and pushed me to excel at whatever I did. Found me the best schools and placed me in training camps and teams for downhill skiing from the time I could stand. At twelve, I went off to boarding school during the year, and offseason training camps for skiing over the summers. When my mother died, my father didn't change a thing. He shipped me back to boarding school the day after her funeral, even though it was still winter break."

Tru's hand darted forward to lace our fingers together. "I'm sorry. That must have been really hard."

It was, and confusing, and isolated. I didn't find out about my mom's affair until I called the detectives to ask about their progress. My father wasn't keeping me informed. It was up to me to follow up until they solved the murder. "My father was a surgeon and spent a lot of time at the hospital. My mother was an attorney and spent a lot of time at the office and on client trips. They were well off, not that they had time to enjoy it." Something I promised myself would never happen to me. I engaged in hobbies, took vacations, and went out with friends. Work may be the main focal point of my life, but I could focus on more than one thing. Until now, until Tru, nothing had motivated me to find another focus.

"That's a trap a lot of people find themselves in," she said in understanding because she seemed to understand everything when it came to human behavior. She also wasn't annoyed by what she must think were disconnected ramblings. She'd let me talk and talk and talk without addressing her question if it would make me more comfortable.

"Anyway, when my mom died, she left her half of the house and all personal property to my dad. Her parents, though, had given their kids most of the proceeds they received when they sold their farm in northern Holland after natural gas reserves were found. My mom kept that money in a separate account, which turned into a trust fund for me." I studied Tru's reaction. No flaring of her pupils, no widening of her eyes, no broadening smile as was always the case whenever someone found out about my trust fund. She showed only concern. "My first clue something wasn't right after my mom died came from the school office when they wanted to confirm my dad's change of address. We lived in a nice neighborhood of Lake Placid, but the new address was in the richest part of town. On top of that, he suddenly had a second address in Manhattan. I tried calling to ask what was going on, but he was always busy. He eventually emailed to tell me he felt like he needed to move out of the house he'd shared with Mom. I wasn't happy about it, but I never spent much time at home anyway. Then, a few months later, a friend from elementary school emailed me a photo of my dad getting out of a Bentley in front of his new mansion. Even when my mother was alive and had access to that kind of money, they didn't spend extravagantly." I pushed out a long breath, still upset I was put in a position where I needed to take action at the age of fifteen. "It was so unlike him I had to ask my mom's estate lawyer to look into the trust. My father was listed as the trustee, which gave him the ability to spend money from the account for my benefit. In seven months, he'd blown through more than half of the trust account."

"Oh, Renske. That's awful." Her hand came up to stroke my arm.

"I was still two years from college. At that rate, I wouldn't have enough to pay for it. When I finally got a hold of him to ask about the spending, he justified everything by saying the house was ours and the apartment would be convenient for when I flew into JFK and the cars were for our transportation. So, in his mind, all of it was for my benefit. I asked him not to spend any more to ensure there'd be enough left for college. He came back with how my mother had made him trustee for a reason." I shrugged, remembering his autocratic response. How he expected me to accept whatever he decided. Anger never factored in. Our relationship wasn't close. I never felt enough for him to become angry. "I asked the lawyer to get an injunction against further spending, and when my father reacted badly to that, I applied for emancipation to take control of my life and what remained of my mother's trust." The proceedings were over in record time once the judge saw how my father had managed my trust and that I'd been at boarding school and summer camps since I was twelve. He could see giving me emancipation wouldn't change my lifestyle or cause undue hardships.

"I'm so sorry you had to go through that." She tilted forward and wrapped her arms around me. She hugged in sympathy and support as much as for elation and connection.

"It was for the best. We were never close, so it wasn't like I would miss a whole lot with him. Plus, to be fair, I reminded him of my mother who hurt him with her affair. He was hurting her back by trying to use up all the money she'd kept separate from their accounts."

"Did you see him while you were in New York? Is that what your trip was about?"

"No, I was meeting with the bank and investment managers of the trust. Even with all the spending, it still paid for boarding school, college, and grad school. After that, I never touched it." Other than to invest the remaining funds, which was a sliver of the original amount. My financial nerdiness couldn't help making investment decisions over the years to help grow the balance past what my grandparents had left to my mother.

"Okay." Her cautious tone said she didn't know where I was going with this.

"I wasn't sure I'd ever use it." Which made me sound crazy, I realize. Who wouldn't use money available to her? Part of it was about not earning the money myself, and another part had to do with guilt surrounding the negative effects of collecting those natural gas deposits. Rationally, I knew they would have been collected whether my grandparents owned the farm or not, but it still felt a tad improper. Charitable contributions helped keep the guilt at bay, and as long as I was satisfied with my career, I'd never need the funds for personal use again. Only one possibility ever crossed my mind, but the circumstances never came up until now. "I get paid enough to live the way I want. I like my work and would have been happy to continue as the resort's CFO."

She nodded and gripped my hands again. "You've probably already checked, but there are some openings in town. The companies aren't as big, obviously, but they could be challenging."

"Thank you, but I have a different idea. One that needs your input." I pushed out a nervous breath. "I'm thinking of making an offer on the resort. I know the financials back and forth, I've been in the industry since I got out of school, and we've analyzed the possible returns on investment. It would be a challenge from the start, but a good one." I tilted my head and gazed at her. She opened and closed her mouth twice, stunned again. "I wouldn't want to move forward without your help, though. I've got the business and finances covered, but the place can't run without people, and that's your expertise."

She made a small sound and jolted out of her stunned state. Her eyes grew watery as they peered into mine. "You're going to stay? If you buy the company, I mean. You'd stay in town?"

My head shook in surprise as I let out a brief chuckle. All the nervousness I'd been feeling oozed away. "You find out I'm rich enough to buy a ski resort, and your only question is whether or not I'll keep living in town?"

She smiled, blinking away the moisture from her eyes. Her fingers came up to caress my cheek. "That's what I care about. You staying. However that happens, I just want you to stay."

My heart started beating double-time. "Yeah? You wouldn't mind if I stuck around for a while longer?"

"I wouldn't mind if you stuck around forever." Her mouth popped open, eyes widening in recognition of what she admitted. Ten seconds passed in her stunned silent state before she fixed a determined gaze on me. Not one bit of regret showed in her gaze, a little embarrassment for blurting it out, maybe, but no regret.

"You are perfection," I whispered a truth that came directly from my heart. No editing, no holding back. "Does this mean you'd stay on to help me run the resort? Help humanize me in the eyes of our employees?"

"You don't need any help humanizing, as you call it."

I scoffed even as I soaked in the elation of having such a strong defender. "They have eighteen different nicknames for me. My favorite is Si, short for Siberian."

A wince pinched her beautiful face. "I'm sorry they can't see you as I do."

"No one sees me like you do."

A brief moment of cockiness showed before her signature humility took over. "Are you sure you want to use your mother's trust to buy a place with employees who didn't appreciate you?"

"There's a lot of potential with the right changes, and going for a CFO spot at another resort would take me away from you. That's not at all what I want."

"You want to stay." She touched my face. "For us?"

"I want to stay for us." For her, because she was so lovely. For me, because having her in my life made it worthy, and for us, because together, nothing seemed impossible.

MURMURS MOVED to an uproar as I came through the kitchen doors into the lodge dining room. Two and a half weeks after Gus held his hey-sorry-we're-fiscal-idiots-and-you're-all-out-of-a-job meeting, the remaining company employees crowded around the tables and spilled into the great room. According to Tru, not everyone wanted to stick around after the mountain closed for another all-staff meeting. The last one hadn't gone so well, but leave it to her to rally everyone to the meeting point.

Not for the first or tenth or hundredth time, awareness of my good fortune settled over me. It had nothing to do with the trust fund arranged by my mother. Nor was it the result of all the hard work put into my career. The most fortunate marvel to happen in my life was getting to know Tru and having her trudge through the miles and miles of remoteness surrounding me to handily trounce me with her optimism.

My eyes swept the crowd. Tru was easy to spot; would forever be easy to spot for me. My heart could find her in every room. Standing at the front beside her coworker Mina, she fought hard to hide the beaming smile that appeared on my arrival. I wasn't much better at veiling the euphoria rushing through me.

"What's Frozen doing here?"

"Who let Icebox back in?"

"Gus bailing on us is bad enough, but he hired Glacial back?"

"For what? We're all out of jobs in six weeks anyway. What's Wintry going to do, take away our office supply money? Make us work double shifts until the place closes?"

That was one way to dampen the euphoria. Step into a room where everyone thought I was a ruthless, pecuniary cyborg. This should be a super fun meeting.

"Why don't you give Renske the chance to tell you before you think the worst," Tru raised her voice to be heard.

Only someone like Tru, esteemed by all her colleagues, could be my advocate and temper their impending riot. I let out a relieved sigh. My heart knew something else where Tru was concerned. Something far more permanent.

Time to focus. It would help if I could see everyone in the room. As much as I disliked the idea of climbing on furniture, my six-foot frame wasn't enough of a height advantage in the crowd. I stepped onto a chair and up onto the nearest table. That brought the buzz in the room to a halt.

"Hello, everyone. Thank you for staying late this evening. For everyone I didn't have a chance to meet while acting as CFO, I'm Renske Van der Valk."

"Where's Gus?"

"Or Aiden?"

"Yeah, what's up with them?" Questions were shouted from all directions.

"The resort has been purchased," I told them, purposely leaving out who had purchased the resort. They might not stay to the end of the meeting if they realized Frozen owned the place. As far as anyone knew, the corporation Penny set up and had negotiated on behalf of bought the resort. "Gus and Aiden have retired. I'll be the new CEO."

Lots of rumbling, too jumbled to make out, but it wasn't hard to guess the general theme. They were confused and upset for the most part, but also a little hopeful.

"So, the mountain's staying open?" someone in the legal department asked.

"It is," I confirmed. "There will be some changes in how we operate, and we're currently in negotiations to sell the inn to a hotelier." Angry shouts, presumably from the hotel staff in the room, sounded. I put up my hands to quell their worries. "The negotiations include keeping on all current staff. No one there will lose their jobs. This was a tough decision, but in the end, we're primarily a ski and snowboarding destination. Innkeeping is a challenging industry made more difficult by the ease of online vacation rentals these days. If the inn wants to stay competitive, it needs a major renovation and organizational expertise to push it to the top of the hotel booking sites. Our efforts should be focused on the industry we're in."

"What about our jobs?" one of the IT staff piped up.

"Some positions will be juggled and all but one level of management may be eliminated, but you'll all have the opportunity to apply for the remaining open positions. For those of you who were ready to leave with the promised layoff package, we'll honor those terms."

Surprised expressions and exclamations came forward in a wave. I might have overestimated their eagerness to keep their jobs and underestimated how much they disliked me. What would I do if everyone gave notice on their way out tonight? I had a huge amount of faith in everything Tru could accomplish, but she and I couldn't run this place alone.

"If you stay on through the end of next month, which was Gus's estimated timeline, and decide you're not happy with our new direction, you'll be given the two-week layoff package promised to you. Employees in eliminated positions can transition to another spot, or you'll be given two weeks plus one week for every year you've been at the company." Considering most of the vice presidents, directors, and managers who hadn't already left were hired within the last two years, an extra two weeks of salary to let them go guilt-free wouldn't break our finances.

"Did you fire Gus and Aiden?"

"They were bought out." Far more generously than they deserved, yet still a drop in the pond compared to their combined salaries. They, alone, made up twenty-five percent of the payroll. Shaving the other unnecessary executives added thirty percent to our profit margin without the need for any other changes.

"Will you be replacing some of the bosses who already left?"

"Not right away. You all know how to do your jobs." Or, on Tru's advice, I could pretend to have confidence in that. Many of them did, but some really did need a supervisor to motivate them. "I'll also be adjusting some salaries based on market research I conducted as the CFO here. Marketing, IT, and legal are all within standards. The remaining departments will see an increase in their paychecks. Also, since most of the women aren't being paid equally, that needs to be rectified."

Various sounds of pleasure rolled through the crowd. More money was always a hit.

"We're also instituting a bonus system tied directly to profits to be paid out each December."

Now there were some cheers. Tru was right, hit them with the positives, and they'll barely remember the negatives.

"Over the next month, we'll start instituting some procedural changes. New employee manuals will be distributed. Many of your questions will be answered then.

I'm asking you to withhold making a decision until you've seen and gotten used to the changes. For now, the purpose of this meeting was to let you know the resort will not be closing and your jobs will continue uninterrupted." I paused for questions, but the surprise announcements seemed to stun them into silence. "I appreciate you staying after hours to attend, and thank you for your commitment to the mountain." Since no questions came at me, I stepped down from the table and headed for the kitchen.

As soon as the door closed, I could hear voices start up. Questions and comments and disbelief came from all parts of the room. They'd be looking for answers, and with almost no managers left, they'd turn to Tru and Mina as the remaining members of the HR department. I wasn't worried about leaving them out there alone. If anyone could quell this crowd, it would be Tru. She could do her job far better than her boss ever could, and she was much admired by her colleagues.

I shouldn't be eavesdropping at the kitchen door, but I couldn't help myself. They seemed less inclined to quit on the spot as when I'd first announced being the new CEO, but more would be leaving. Some people could never get past their initial biases.

"What the hell, Tru? Mina? Do you guys know how this happened?"

"Yeah, what are we supposed to do?"

"What really happened to Gus and Aiden?"

"Frozen is probably holding them hostage in her ice cave."

"That's enough!" Tru's voice rose above the others, and even I jumped in place at her forcefulness. "That woman you've done nothing but insult from day one was tasked with making all the tough decisions Gus and Aiden were too ineffective to implement on their own. Even then, they rarely followed her advice, which is why the company was going bankrupt."

"Tru's right," Mina spoke just as loudly, and I felt myself nod in approval. "Carly told us some stuff before she left. Gus and Aiden knew they were going to lose the business, and instead of paying money to the bank to keep us open long enough to get through another winter season, they bought snowmobiles, and a shuttle, and spent thirty grand on a party. As uptight as we might think Renske is, she was right about that party. And I'd rather have a job working for someone a little standoffish, than not have a job because a friendly boss ran the business into the ground." Not exactly a ringing endorsement, but she sounded wholly on my side. She also sounded like she wouldn't mind being tasked with finding buyers for the new snowmobiles and shuttle we'd never use, which would strike one item off my immediate to-do list.

"And by the way," Tru took up the torch again. "Renske is aware of all the nasty little names you have for her. She's heard you use every hurtful one, and she hasn't fired anyone for it. How about we give her a second chance? She just saved your jobs and hasn't asked for anything in return. Now, go home. We start fresh with a new big boss tomorrow."

It took ten minutes before Tru pushed her way through the kitchen doors. She broke into a smile when she saw me waiting in the empty space. In seconds, she was in my arms.

"You were brilliant," she complimented.

"You managed to assure them when I couldn't." I hugged her tight, still not used to being able to hold her whenever I wanted. "Thanks for sticking up for me."

She leaned back and smiled brightly. "You're worth sticking up for, and don't you forget it."

Not possible. Not when just the sight of her reminded me how lucky I was.

The Following Christmas Day

WARM LIPS brushed against the back of my neck as arms circled my waist. Heat surrounded me, not that I should be surprised. I hadn't felt cold since this amazing woman enveloped me in her life.

"We're not taking it down tonight." The husky voice sent shivers through me.

I reached back and brought Tru around to press against my front. "You can keep it up as long as you like."

"Really? You like your first Christmas tree that much?" Tru's probing look was cautious. Her concern was one of the things I loved best about her.

"It smells nice." I couldn't let her know I was a complete Christmas convert just yet. She'd think I was too easy.

"You love it," she teased, leaning in and waiting, her face tilted upward.

I stared at that beautiful face and tantalizing mouth. I should make her wait, but I was under no illusion I had the upper hand with her. I may technically be her boss at work, but she was my partner in every sense. Leaning down, I captured her mouth in a kiss that left us both breathless.

"I love *you*," I stressed, still not conceding that I liked anything to do with Christmas.

She flashed her dimples at me. "I love you, too."

"With Blythe over at Jolie's for lunch, we have a little time to ourselves today." Especially since I'd followed her advice to close the resort for the day. Too many employees objected to working the day, giving Tru's department a headache it didn't need.

Her hands moved up my back, tingles sparked in their wake. "Are you thinking of catching up on some of the sleep Blythe interrupted this morning for gift opening, or something a little more fun?"

I took in a deep breath, closing my eyes. Bliss still took me by surprise. Moments like this happened nearly every day, and still, unexpected bliss. "We'll definitely get to that."

"Now, maybe?" Her dimples flashed and my heart thudded.

"Soon, for sure. Right now, I want to show you your Christmas present."

"What?" She pulled back in surprise. "You already gave me a present this morning. I love my new ski equipment, by the way, in case I haven't mentioned it a hundred times already."

"You have." I chuckled, remembering the twin squeals from the sisters when she unwrapped her skis, boots, poles, and helmet.

"I've never had new skis or poles before. Never. We always got our equipment from the ski swap."

"You said." I skated my hand up to stroke her neck. "I'm glad you like them."

"I love them. Thank you. We were supposed to stick to limits, if you'll remember."

I shrugged, not feeling any guilt for breaking their rule. She was lucky I didn't buy her a new car for her birthday in March last year. Only the fact that she was saving part of the raise she got when she took over as HR director to buy a new SUV kept me from getting it for her. I'd eventually follow their rules after a few more years of spoiling her and her sister. It wasn't like Tru followed the guideline, either. She added to my overcoat collection with a dapper calf-length trench as her gift to me.

"So, no more presents." She tried to sound stern, but her expression softened immediately. "I have everything I could ever want now that you're in my life."

I tipped forward, pressing my lips to hers. She kissed like no other, raw wanting mixed with tender devotion. I woke up every day craving them. "I'm the blessed one, please know that." My fingers traced from her dimple across her cheek and along the shell of her ear. "This present is for us, all of us."

"You got something for our family?"

My eyes misted every time she called us that. It had been so long since I felt any family ties, but Tru and Blythe made sure I'd never forget the feeling ever again. "House plans." I waved a hand toward the roll of paper tied with a red bow now sitting under the tree.

"House...? Hey, where did that come from?"

I bent to pick it up and handed it to her. "I have my ways."

She untied the bow and rolled out the poster sized sheet of paper onto the dining room table. A four-bedroom house plan was sketched out before her. Her eyes widened as she studied the plan. She traced some of the lines with her elegant fingers before looking up at me. "A house?"

"I know you and Blythe love this place. I do, too." Having moved in about a month ago, I was getting used to the tighter space as much as I was getting used to sharing my life with Tru. "If you'd both rather stay here, we'll stay. This plan gives us more room inside and out. Guest rooms for your family to visit and Blythe's friends to stay over. Or, kids' rooms if we decide that's in the cards for us."

Her brow spiked. We'd talked about kids in abstracts only. She wasn't certain yet, and I knew I'd be okay with whatever she decided. I never thought I'd want kids. On my own, I definitely wouldn't, but with Tru, it could be a wonderful experience. "You've given this some thought."

"I want us to have everything we might need. Space for your family to stay and a whole wing for Blythe to design however she likes. You don't have to sell this place. Keep it for when more of your family visits all at once, or use it as a vacation rental. Blythe may decide she'd like to move in here if she gets married one day." I gripped Tru's chin, trying to impart all the possibilities this move could make for us. "Or she could decide she'd rather live with us full-time in the new house at some point, with or without a spouse. Whatever she wants. Whatever you want. I just think we need a little more room. Neither of us has enough closet space, and you can barely turn around without smacking something in Blythe's bathroom."

"Oh, Renske," Tru whispered, her eyes moving from mine to the plans and back. "You've thought of everything." She turned and buried her face in my neck, arms coming around me.

"It's a lot of change. We haven't lived together long. Is it too much all at once?"

"I love that you're worried about a wonderful gift, but you think nothing of all the changes you're trying to accomplish at work. All the spinning plates you already have going to make the resort exceptional. How can you think about taking on another project?"

"I've been planning what I'd do to perfect a resort ever since I started working at them. It's nothing more than finding the right people to complete the steps." We'd hired an exceptional project manager to deal with the construction projects on the resort grounds. The ski-through coffee stand and relocation of the indoor coffee square were handled efficiently and without need for input beyond the initial design meeting. Currently, she was working on remodeling the corporate office to give everyone additional workspace and privacy. Her next project would turn one of the supply buildings onsite into a seasonal staff dormitory, which Tru was jazzed about because it would make her recruiting efforts much easier.

"It's a lot more than that."

"What I mean is I don't need to spend time thinking about those improvements anymore." I tapped a knuckle on the house design. "This is all about my life with you. I haven't had as much time to make extensive plans, but it will never be too much."

She pushed forward, lips grazing my throat, climbing my chin to caress my mouth. Long, luscious moments later, she ended her exploration. "Did I mention I'm completely hooked on you?"

I felt my face split into a smile. "You might have. I'm equally hooked, Truly." Enough that I've ordered a custom engagement ring to be ready for Valentine's day. It might be cliché, but I fell for a woman who loves holidays. All of them.

Her dimples flared. "That's the best gift you'll ever give me, Renske."

"But a new house ranks pretty high, doesn't it?" I laughed when she made a so-so gesture with her hand. I tapped the drawing. "This is just a placeholder design. We'll meet with an architect to go over what we all want from a new house."

"Blythe is going to love the process, but we're going to have a serious talk about how we'll fund this build." She raised two fingers and pressed them against my mouth. "We are. No debate. We're in this together, on everything."

I couldn't argue with that, and more importantly, I didn't want to. She could demand anything of me, and I'd gladly give it. "We are, and this'll be fun." A lot more work than fun, but the end result will make life easier for us.

She poked me in the ribs. "It will be." Her mouth came in for another kiss.

"You've convinced me."

"That's right. I don't want you going back to your Frozen ways."

My heart thumped at the teasing reminder of the nearly forgotten nickname. Not quite abolished, but not freely bandied about anymore. Most of the employees appreciated the changes and welcomed the improvements. Tru worked her magic with the staff and managed to make me seem more approachable. I was still the big boss who had to make some unpopular decisions, but no one has openly accused me of being an ice queen in months.

I reached to cup her cheek, thumb dipping into the dimple that appeared. "Never again, my love. Not with your warmth keeping the cold away."

Having learned to ski at a young age, Lynn Galli doesn't take warmth or comfort for granted. She's never again felt the kind of cold she used to experience while riding chairlifts in the bitter wind and sleeting snow, nor the discomfort of ankles and shins rubbed raw in ski boots, toes frozen solid, and fingers barely able to bend after her gloves failed to stay dry. Happy now to live in a relatively mild winter climate, Lynn keeps those unpleasant sensations locked away until she stupidly writes yet another story set in a ski town.

VIRGINIA CLAN

AT LAST (PREQUEL) – Willa Lacey never thought acquiring five million in venture capital for her software startup would be easier than suppressing romantic feelings for a friend. Having never dealt with either situation, Willa finds herself torn between what she knows and what could be.

WASTED HEART (BOOK 1) – Attorney Austy Nunziata moves across the country to try to snap out of the cycle of pining for her married best friend. Despite knowing how pointless her feelings are, five months in the new city hasn't seemed to help. When she meets FBI agent, Elise Bridie, that task becomes a lot easier.

IMAGINING REALITY (BOOK 2) – Changing a reputation can be the hardest thing anyone can do, even among her own friends. But Jessie Ximena has been making great strides over the past year to do just that. Will anyone, even her good friends, give her the benefit of the doubt when it comes to finding a forever love?

BLESSED TWICE (BOOK 3) – Briony Gatewood has considered herself a married woman for fifteen years even though she's spent the last three as a widow. Her friends have offered to help her get over the loss of her spouse with a series of blind dates, but only a quiet, enigmatic colleague can make Briony think about falling in love again.

FOREVERMORE (BOOK 4) - M Desiderius never thought she could have a normal life filled with love. She gets all that and more when she marries Briony, including an amazing foster daughter named Olivia. Every wish she'd never allowed herself to voice became real. When someone from Olivia's past threatens M's newfound family, can she carry on in the face of loss or will it push her back into a life of solitude?

ASPEN FRIENDS

MENDING DEFECTS (BOOK 1) – Small town life for Glory Eiben has always been her ideal. With her rare congenital heart defect, keeping family and friends close by preserves her easygoing attitude. When Lena Coleridge moves in next door, life becomes anything but easy. Lena is a reluctant transplant and even more reluctant friend. Their growing friendship adds many layers to Glory's ideal.

SOMETHING SO GRAND (BOOK 2) – A designer for the wealthy, Vivian Yeats doesn't have time for relationships, yet she longs for romance. She's had to settle in the past when it comes to women but won't bother to again. If romance is going to happen for her, it'll take someone special to turn her head. Natalie Harper, the new contractor on her jobsites, might just be the woman to do it.

LIFE REWIRED (BOOK 3) – Two years ago, Molly Sokol decided she wanted to get serious about finding that special someone. She could picture her perfectly—petite, feminine, excitable, adoring, and ultra-affectionate. When the opposite of all that comes along in the form of Falyn Shaw, Molly never thought they'd be anything more than friends. Being wrong has never felt so good.

OTHER ROMANCES

UNCOMMON EMOTIONS – When someone spends her days ripping apart corporations, compartmentalization is key. Love doesn't factor in for Joslyn Simonini. Meeting Raven Malvolio ruins the harmony that Joslyn has always felt, introducing her to passion for the first time in her life.

FULL COURT PRESSURE – The pressure of being the first female basketball coach of a men's NCAA Division 1 team may pale in comparison to the pressure Quinn Viola feels in her unexpected love life.

ONE-OFF – Weddings have never been Skye MacKinnon's thing. When she's put in charge of planning her friend's big event, she's less than thrilled. Finding out she'll have to work with the bane of her college existence, Ainsley Baird, may push her right over the edge. Knowing there's nothing she can do to change her circumstances or the company she'll have to keep, her only plan is to make it through the happy occasion without setting fire to the whole show or one person in particular.

CLICHÉD LOVE –As a journalist, Vega spends her days writing other people's stories. For her latest assignment, she's taking down LGBT love stories and worrying that her eyes might roll right out of their sockets during every mushy interview. Only the help of her new friend, Iris, who also believes romance stories are worth mocking, prevents her from finding ways to make her subjects mysteriously disappear to save her from having to listen to more clichés.

OUT OF ORDER – Lindsay St. James spends her days fixing political problems. No problem too taxing, no issue too complex to resolve for someone who dedicates herself to her career. When she stumbles into a judicial bribery scheme affecting her political candidate, she has to rely on the help of the newest and most distracting member of the judiciary. For the first time, her personal interests are keeping her from focusing on her profession, and she doesn't seem all that bothered about it.

WINTER CALLING – As a human resources coordinator for a ski resort, Tru's biggest challenge is finding people to take the job seriously. The new CFO definitely fits that characterization. A little too well, according to Tru's colleagues. Her stoic demeanor makes them believe she's a cold, unfeeling android. Always willing to think the best of people, Tru sets out to discover if Renske is really as imperturbable as she seems.

CPSIA information can be obtained
at www.ICGtesting.com
Printed in the USA
BVOW08s0635280118
506478BV00001B/47/P